BECKETT'S LAST ACT

Mora Grey

Beckett's Last Act

M
P
MUSWELL PRESS

Beckett's Last Act
© 2014 Mora Grey

First published by Muswell Press Ltd, 6 Pinchin Street, London E1 1SA

The rights of Mora Grey to be identified as the author of this work has been asserted in accordance with Section 77 of the Copyright, Design and Patents Act 1988.

All rights reserved. No part of this publication may be reproduced, stored in a retrieval system or transmitted in any form or by any means electronic, mechanical, photocopying, recording or otherwise without the permission of the publisher of this book.

All characters and events in this publication, other than those clearly in the public domain, are fictitious and any resemblance to real persons, living or dead, is purely coincidental.

A CIP record of this book is available from The British Library.

ISBN 978-0-9928171-0-7

Text designed by Hand & Eye Letterpress
Cover designed by Barney Beech

Typeset in ITC Galliard

Printed and bound by
Shortrun Press, Sowton Industrial Estate, Bittern Road, Exeter EX2 7LW

For Esme

Prologue

JESSE'S DREAM

A dream emerges from that royal road, the universal unconscious. It is a common dream, as common as muck. I am in the theatre anticipating a part that resembles hell. Playwright Samuel Beckett is on stage discussing one of the two plays to be performed. The director, designer and two young lovers particularly stand out. The assembled company struggle to meet his expectations. A large clock hangs above the proscenium arch. Time is running out. I experience an aroused elevated feeling alongside deflated apprehension. I ask the designer, a woman, to tell me what is going on. Her voice, rhythmic plainsong, replies.

'Nothing much happens, each play has one character, a man and a woman. Both are reminiscing in different ways. In *Not I* the woman speaks out her life in fragments in a matter of minutes. Twelve to be precise. It is hard to catch the words, she talks so fast that you mainly catch a mood shot with pain and anxiety, only her mouth visible on stage. The man in *Krapp's Last Tape* is about to make a recording of his thoughts about the previous year. He does this on each of his birthdays. He listens to the older tapes to prepare himself.'

The designer's description appears as words tumbling from a page, hanging in the air. They are fully formed, calligraphic shapes, solid groups of sounds. I stand straining to hear and see every word and feel myself moved and alert to their content, wanting to know more.

MORNING PREPARATION

1. The Theatre Stalls

VIRGINIA THE DESIGNER

The sets have been put up overnight and the flats are secured, so I have placed myself at the back of the stalls for the moment. People will find me if they need me, but I need a bit of mental space where it is quiet and I'm not necessarily seen. Everyone is unusually on edge, including myself. We are faced with the simplest problems on the face of it. It is the last day of rehearsals. The day of the technical and dress rehearsal and a first performance and we are finishing off, putting everything in its final place. I can only hope something evolves that helps the general atmosphere, which is oddly doom-laden, but waiting for the world to turn feels a little like hell. Peter, myself, Sam, and even the crew are all wandering around in a state of puzzlement. As if all this work is going to be for nothing. So much effort and endeavour reaching its final stage and yet there is huge tension and agitation combined with an air of grim resignation and flatness. I wonder why we are all sleepwalking. Is it a virus? We all look extremely well, if more than a little anxious, distracted and closed off. We are seen to be doing as much as we can of what is asked, and yet so much still needs to settle. We are walking through one of the plays as if it had been played a thousand times and it is dead for us. We are not suffering enough, there seems to be little adrenalin around, and all the attachment, friendliness and love for the play has disappeared. If I, too, angrily begin to suspect there is nothing in the heads of those around me, that everyone has dissociated from the work, that they are not giving one hundred percent at this point, I am bound to feel it as a slight. Peter leaks frustration. George looks unhappy and uncomfortable and who can blame him? He has been completely ignored by Sam. Sam continues to be remote, except with Anna. If anything is said to George by Peter that appears critical, him ,he looks hurt and puzzled and says 'let's try again.' He is good – extremely good – and yet there is nothing alive available today. He is unreachable, nothing seems to shock him into making himself known. Even a sudden, seemingly unprovoked outburst from Peter, 'Wake up, George!' simply left George startled, angry and then noticeably depressed. Sam has refused to engage with either Peter or George for some time now, which is hurtful and hugely irritating, as it is causing such unnecessary conflict and apprehension. George is taking the brunt, which is unfair and, most importantly, unhelpful. He has had enormous success and knows he was cast because he will draw the crowds, so may be forgiven for being confused that he is being marginalised. He is used to taking charge in his performances as he is a large presence and this is not being taken into consideration. But when I try to approach Sam on the subject, he simply makes it plain that this is not an area for discussion.

As usual when stuck, I find myself going over everything to see if something can rise up from forensic examination. We are working on two plays, *Krapp's Last Tape* and *Not I*. At the beginning, each of the two characters was a new child, a couple of fraternal twins, one male, one female, each the only character in the separate plays. The woman, Anna, needs less help from me as there is literally nothing visible on the stage, no costume, no set, just blackout. Only her mouth is visible, so there are interesting practical tasks to solve. She does need me to recognise that she is suffering because of the level of emotional pressure, an anxiety made from too many compressed emotions flowing through her at any of the long moments on stage. And her young daughter is seriously ill. I have to keep an eye on her in case she starts to become overwhelmed. Sam has pushed and pushed her going over the script night after night, until we had to intervene on her behalf and ask that the stage manager, Jane, take over in the evening as Anna was beginning to be overcome by his persistence and perfectionism. He did agree to this and apologised. An enormous relief.

And one particular end-of-days old man was bringing unfamiliar worlds, presenting me with a new set of challenges. As Proust would have it, occupying in time and in mind a much greater place than is so sparingly given us in space. I would never mistake Krapp, Sam's alter-ego, now, as some do, as a broken old fart, a repulsive specimen. He is in his late sixties but he is facing up to the dark and light forces in the world, can speak directly to us about this and is fascinating, his language unsurpassed. I have an endless capacity and fascination for brilliant difficult minds in men. And he is also suffering because of failure. He is an artist for whom everything has been stripped away. Everything on stage has to reflect that all that is superfluous in life had been given up. There is so much to admire and sympathise with in a man who has come to this point of the journeyman's life. I have always been attracted to the curmudgeonly mixed with the intellectual and a sense of humour; a jocular free mind attached to the negative rather than the positive. So I was going to give him a beautiful sketch of a set, every element in it just so, but more so. The problems he presented me with needed to be decently furnished; the subtleties of his dark, broody character and the lightness and delicate rhythm of his language; constant and repetitive. Yes, there had been the challenge of making something exciting and stimulating between us. Anything is possible with new obsessions, new loves. His setting demanded a careful and ruthless paring down of content. But not the expectations; those are never to be given up. So I gave him the simplest background: black material, screening his man's room and interior world. No distractions from what he is thinking and doing. Allowing the director and me, his temporary guardians, to see and hear his naked presence in Krapp and experience with him a stripping away of ourselves. Some familiar emotional demands could be met and responses repeated, having met this kind of difficult character before, and knowing what this singular, incorrigible temperament looks like. I could make it the cut of his hair and the worn, shapelessness of his silhouette. At my age, as men young and old are well-worn territory, I can also use some old reliable solutions, the visual texture of the threadbare and the careworn.

This old man's mind is closing around the essentials of his life. It is a time of looking back, not forward. He listens to the tapes recorded on his birthdays in previous years. Memories may be recorded, but are not fixed. As they are worked on each year, critically, reassessed, they are re-recorded, remade Promethean memory. It is not only the tapes that are scrutinised over the decades. He also pours over the ledgers he keeps alongside the tapes to log them. They are another register of attempts to capture time, thoughts, feelings, the essences of events; an index of the tapes, which record key details, or perhaps transcripts of resonate passages, which are prompts to painful, heartbreaking and revelatory times. I found old books, with the weight of archaeology, to be the prop ledgers. When you pick the books up and feel the weight of their serious depth of scholarship you can imagine they carry memory for all time. Once he has read the ledgers and listened to short bursts of the tapes, you should see the immense draining effort. He becomes gasping, ravenously thirsty and hungry. Emotional and intellectual hunger arises in him and is made visible for us and with it the greedy reaching for wine and bananas. According to Sam, bananas are the particular sustenance (manna) suited both to the young baby and the aged. I'm quite partial to a banana myself, though I have come a long way from babyhood and have a stretch of time to go before I catch up with Sam's or his character Krapp's longevity.

Like a new child rapidly putting ideas together, the old man shows me that memory is not fixed. It is constantly reworked, always renewed from the present perspective. He seems to appreciate how serious and mentally treacherous this exploration is. His anticipation and anxiety are justified, as is his stock of fortifying wine in the store offstage at the back. His birthday task has to be approached in a slow, brave, measured fashion. He is completely alone. He can only face himself alone and he can be forgiven the need for a little bolstering with a drink or two.

The aesthetic fabric which makes up the warp and weft of Krapp's situation must be made from the right cloth. Fine weaving will give me, the company and crew, and the audience, a lot of pleasure. This character's work is to show his essential nature: absorbing, frightening, deadening, lively, comic, compelling and exasperating. Yet I missed much of this when I read his first play. I simply did not know how he, Sam, could write about such a dark desolate part of a life and not want to kill himself, until I realised that the words, the rhythm and the silences are what makes us whole. Is it the ageing, disintegrating, harsh and bitter side of Krapp in ascendency in people's minds? May George not have understood this and be frightened of being killed off by the play? Even Anna is in a high state of fear and anxiety, beside herself with worry. All the men are acting as if they would like to kill each other, and all of us! Everyone is cutting each other out, guarded and closed, not able to take up the care and attention shown by the crew and me. But, despite this, I have to keep asking myself, what more can be done?

As the designer I can only repeatedly go over what I have made for the actors, particularly for Krapp. I must oversee all the construction. Even the simplest set of instructions can be misunderstood. I have designed a colourless space (for the most part) which will reflect all the light back. The stage is to give no relief to the eye, most seeking an expanse to drift upon. The intent is to force the viewers back on themselves. I've made small concessions. I have allowed Krapp's desk to have facets, the wood carved so it catches light straying from the spotlights; its angularity enhanced by being the only large object available where the light can do its business. I would have liked something Arts and Crafts or even Catholic Pugin, but I reined these thoughts in. This would be unnecessarily ornate. Instead, the old desk has enough craft to convey a sense of true, albeit abstract, purpose. The recorder and the tape spools all bear the marks of some engineer's care and attention, now worn and battered with use and weary history. George's character can feel the weight of time in these objects. His large pocket watch will physically pull on him: time weighing him down as he sits in his chair or struts about within the confines of his self-imposed restrictions.

I spent long hours on the costumes, choosing each item as I might my own wedding dress. Each character's costume is given ceremonial importance. The clothes have to be tormented, made wretched, distressed, made to look lived in and worn – worn out in this case. I have spent long hours fitting them around the contours of the actors and I can feel more than a little pissed off if they don't appreciate my work. I would never show this, of course. I look at the boots and think how much I have enjoyed them – it took some work to make them look as if they have had a lifetime's wear and are barely holding together. Perhaps they have had two lifetimes' wear, having already been dead man's shoes. I found them in a junk shop. The searching for and finding the character – an essence, a single identity – is supported by this costume, alongside the setting for the play and its make-believe environment. The costume is drawn and painted, and redrawn, as the director, designer (and in this case the writer) look and decide if it nearly resembles the person evolving in the text. This carries on until the satisfactory image, one gauged by emotional responses, arises. If the director says he wants something and I'm not sure why, I will accept this if it continues to be important to him. I know if something is right by how it feels. There is no better gauge or barometer. The actors, of course, like to have drawings – not an indulgence at all. The attention and concentrated reworking will bring results imbued with activity. So much thought and work has gone into each small detail. Thoughtlessness and randomness would not achieve anything near. You can always sense this when presented with a finished object that has the marks of many hours' consideration, without knowing why it touches and stimulates your senses.

Materials serve simplicity of order and can only be used if they assist the writer and actors; structures creating light and shadows make an interior having nothing to do with exterior reality and everything to do with poetry. The lighting serves to highlight all these different areas. I would sit back with the deepest satisfaction watching continuing work on the set – Jerry the lighting man working his magic – if I did not feel so distraught about the company. I know George understands the work he is part of, just how deep it cuts. But at the moment I, too, can find myself having unreasonable thoughts about his performance. He seems to be trying too hard, putting everything into the performance but looking at odds with himself and feeling at odds with the two men who are essential to him right now. However, this is unfair; he is dedicated to his task but has been abandoned by Sam and strangely unnerved since arriving in the theatre. Peter asked me to make a mask to stimulate George's resources, forcing him in on himself. But it is way, way too late for that kind of gradual preparation. It does not address the seriousness of the rupture that, frankly, Sam has created.

2. The Theatre Stalls

PETER THE DIRECTOR

I'm furious. At any point I could spill out. How could a play get so far down the line to find it had the wrong energy? On top of it all I'm feeling hot and feverish. I have probably got the flu but I'm determined to try to ignore it. I don't feel nauseous or achy but this heat seems to come from inside me, my marrow seems to be boiling. My mother recently said this to me: 'You seem to be describing menopausal symptoms, darling. You're a man in your fifties, not a woman, sweetie.' She said this to *me*! How helpful is that? Actually I do feel like a dame, a comic-real hermaphrodite. I'm sweating like a drying out slab of women and woke up in bed in the same state last night. I can see others notice my watery state. But I defy anyone to mention it. If I get a sympathetic look, the tension and anger this causes me soon makes them back off. My pallor is alarming. I saw it in the mirror and it gave me an additional turn. At least remembering this made me smile. Otherwise, sitting in the dark of the stalls, keeping my distance, I am a director who is failing, with a director's mask cut from both *Commedia dell'arte* and Ancient Greek tragedy. Virginia could not make me a better one. I want her to make me a facsimile so I can use it when I want to malevolently disturb the actors, and myself. I am Anguish, Rage, Disappointment and Carnival personified. I am a version of Sam's character but the only one thus far to be found in the theatre. The play is not meant to be a dreary domestic tragedy. It is meant to be unnerving, disturbing, grievous yes, but riveting and hopefully funny at times. At the moment it is a travesty, and it's my fault, as the buck stops with me. I am feeling both anger and hate towards the situation, and myself, as it's my responsibility. Let's hope this experience has a transforming element. It feels bloody elemental, fire and ice, both fiery ice-cold water and fierce heat, but I'm not cooling off.

Is it really too late to ask Virginia to make a mask for George? Anna does not need one, as she is completely shrouded, body and head, throughout her performance because language and the emotion it provokes are what are important here, not the beautiful actors' faces. A death mask meant to help carry the thoughts and words of embitterment and determination? A comic mask to complement and switch to when going through the absurd daily rituals? Wearing a mask where there is no living face to hide behind means that a whole range of feelings are trapped inside and mediated by it, helping the actor to find everything inside himself. Could she do this for him? Would she if I insisted? But of course it's too bloody late. We have only this day to go, with the dress rehearsal later, followed by a performance. It's too late for any improvisational experiment. If only I'd thought of it earlier, but I didn't. I can see that George is drawing on his whole repertoire and armoury and has been incredibly hurt that this is not what is wanted. He is a King Actor and not used to being asked to subsume himself.

I wanted the actors to feel extremes of consciousness that seem, to their characters to be truer than any so-called normal states. Inner reality is a hell hole, a resonant pit where new energies are formed. I see George trying to meet me, bewildered at times, unhappy. I cannot communicate what I want from him at this stage and I am extremely frustrated with myself. Anna, on the other hand, working steadily with Sam is taking herself to the extreme, carried along by their platonic love affair. She can inhabit the text and make it work, though it is costing her dear. She has struggled with these plays of Sam's, the enormous demands and challenges, a number of times already. But in *Not I*, her part is particularly severe and testing because she's trapped inside herself in the dark with nothing to support her as the experience of madness goes around in her head, the sound of her own voice shattering her equilibrium. Virginia told me that she is watching Anna with some anxiety. She is a woman on the verge of a nervous breakdown. We both understand that only she can pull herself through. Still, she has Sam on her side. At times he, even with her, wants more and more. I, too, want blood. I want her to go mad. Please, more madness, more real madness, a presence of alien, other worldliness, a world of feeling in which every semblance of purpose is stripped away. This is also what Sam wants for the plays, for the actors and audience to be pushed into the most raw, rarest of emotional experiences. Why has he also dismissed me from his attention? He puts me in the category of letting him down. Pretty annoying, but these splits happen. I've had worse.

Even so, where, for fuck's sake, is all this anger coming from? I'm plugged into some pit in myself. It feels like an endless source of terrible intense feeling, a bottomless self-feeding furnace. There's no sense of it coming to an end. It has an endless supply of energy. I have hit an international, no, cosmic, grid. I feel it could keep me alive forever; immortal, smouldering, embers hot and always ready to ignite. It probably will give me the gift of old age, or at least help fire the genes, or destroy them. The trouble at present is that it is too hot and I cannot trust it. No judgement would be uncontaminated by it. Everyone feels separate from me, alien and unavailable. In turn I loathe myself and then everyone else. Only Virginia is exempt from it, but I never would be able to tell her about it. There is no speech or communication in this state. I suppose she must see it. It will stand out in her special field, her sixth sense. She is keeping her distance. Who can blame her?

Sitting in the auditorium my body starts to feel outsized, like a gigantic baby, a grotesque, distorted figure. I am towering above my seat, which I've outgrown. It feels a number of sizes too small, like squeezing into too tight trousers. My face feels pale and blank, eyes darkened holes. My mouth, if I opened it, another gaping orifice. I am neither male nor female – de-sexed. With the production slipping out of my grasp, I've not felt anything remotely libidinal for weeks. My clothes feel damp and stuck to my body and I want to tear them off, and then streak through the auditorium. This would be amusing and I chuckle. I look around. No one seems to be taking any notice of me. Running amok naked, why not? I want to project this hallucinatory image of myself into the play, into George. At least it seems to be the right kind of image – the whole edifice of the play stripped down into one dominant feeling – rage. At this point, nearing disaster, I need to be able to think straight, to look hard at what is happening, but I too am out of it.

Have I trapped myself into some need to create a monstrous Krapp? I wanted to bring out an underlying malevolence alongside the grotesque comedy. Am I losing it? I have never felt so identified with an aspect of a character before in this way. And to be honest I am not so sure it has anything to do with the character. Is it nothing to do with the play? I've been feeling dissatisfied with my lover lately. He is not what I had hoped for. He is without ambition. That's not true. He has ambition but not the kind or amount of ambition I want for him. He is kind and loving towards me, and weak in my eyes. He needs people too much, fluid and conduit, copper-like in his dealing with others. Am I seeing George in this way? No, that would definitely miscast him. George is usually completely sure of himself, although he cannot be feeling that at the moment.

I like company, good company: witty, intelligent, but only when I have done with everything else. I don't really need people as such. I can take them or leave them. The constant of the theatre company, the actors, means I'm never lonely. As I move from one company to another I meet a new family group. This theatre has been a family branch for years. In between times there are enough people around with which to have interesting times. Sex is easy to arrange, if you really want it. Feeling at odds with my dear lover may, I suppose, be connected to falling out at the moment. Falling out with him and potentially everyone around me.

He had said I was without empathy, unable to be with another's suffering. This hurt me. It may be true. I am a man who does what he wants and only that. I try never to do what I don't want to do and am singular in this way. Does this really mean I have no empathy? I don't think so. I would never question someone to see what they felt or thought. I expect others to show themselves. If they did not do so they could not be part of a creative milieu. Well, I did ask Sam about his thoughts earlier, but I'd never pursue it. What would be the point? The person would only give answers unattached to the core of themselves. I feel this is the mark of a developed individual, someone I can work or live with. I do not want to merge with another. I find the idea repulsive. It would threaten to destroy my integrity. To be taken over by another's world is to lose oneself and any possible vision.

I talked to Sam's wife yesterday. A strong, determined French woman, dressed conservatively in the French couture fashion. When I admired her dress and bolero she said she'd made both. Reading between the lines I understand she usually comes to see the shows when they open to give her critique. She picked up the situation immediately. Over a glass of bad French wine, which she politely put to one side, she said Sam was not a good judge of character and tended to make close friends of dubious actors and directors. I took this to mean, as he was not friends with me at the moment, then I must be OK.

The people around me are the least of my problems. I am still out of control in this rather fantastic dissociated state. I can still feel my body morphing and am now even more of a huge omnipotent baby, all at once magically powerful, exciting and threatening. An image of my experience had oddly been described to me previously. A friend once told me a dream about a baby which I have never forgotten. The baby in her dream was huge and a fantastic performer, an incredible gymnast. The lights are dark and the extraordinary, if slightly malevolent baby is in the spotlight in a circus tent. Her analyst pointed out the connection to her pregnancy, obvious enough. Her unconscious was throwing up all kinds of ideas about the baby to come. The baby was represented as a fabulous artist, full of life already, with a healthy developing shadow side.

These associations compound my own physical and mental state. I still feel Gargantuan. I fantasise about tackling George in a duel. If I terrify George I may make him come alive in the way I need him to. He's not complacent, trying hard enough from his own powerful perspective. He deserves to be petrified out of his wits. I rise out of my seat and if anyone cared to notice they would see that I am twenty feet tall. I march up the aisle, a demonic God-like Fury stalking my prey. In reality I have no idea how I'm going to engage with George, to convey the need for more faith in me and the resonances in the words; to allow me to enable him to take more risks and encounter more inner life. I am working up to it. But my thoughts, a logjam inside me, only threaten to make things worse.

3. The Theatre Wardrobe

SAM THE PLAYWRIGHT

I must have slept deeply. I needed to distance myself from what is going on and the feelings of disappointment that continue to threaten me to the point of annihilation. I dreamt the painter Bram van Velde, my dearest friend and the man most akin to me, was playing Krapp. He was wearing a black and white clown's costume made of white diamonds and black jet. A cosmic battle raged through his being, the gems pulsating light and dark. Old Nick stood behind him, disguised as a stagehand, head to toe in blacks that make him almost invisible. I am unable to speak, knowing Bram is in danger and that words cannot help him. I am heartbroken by his predicament. He didn't open them, but his eyes focused on me, two black burning coals all seeing, penetrated by fear and hatred, yet I know he is full of felicity and acceptance.

Exhausted by my dream, my tired half-open eyes take in the room where I'm sitting. Sight and sounds are clear and distinct, and at the same time distant. The old leather armchair is comfortable, a bed folding itself around me. I gradually allow other shapes to come into focus. Momentarily the image of the work going on downstairs comes into my mind but I decide to banish this. Feelings of bewilderment and betrayal can still be hot in me. They are partly directed at myself.

I turn my attention to the dimensions of the space in which I have placed myself after escaping the painful chaos downstairs. Does the room seem smaller or larger because it contains so much? There's a lot of clutter. I won't let that disturb me or press on my active consciousness. Clutter gets in the way of form created by empty space, blotting out essential aspects of experience if you let it, and I need a clearing at this moment. Scanning the room, I'm aware of a shift up to the right so that the whole room slopes to the left. I take in the room at this angle; it is as if the whole building has tilted, and yet all the contents, including myself, remain upright. The outlines of the machines in front of me, and a woman sitting at a sewing machine, are as if suspended. There is an open door on the right creating another distorted rectangle, a quadrangle with large side outwards, which gives permission to further scan from my perspective, audience left to right, the visual components of my geographic position. I start to lose my feelings of unevenness and to feel calm, detached.

The young woman is markedly still, her head slightly bowed over her work. She is sewing, bent, her hair obscures her face and only her hands make a steady rhythmic movement. I have an anxiety about her reddened shiny hair getting caught in the machine. The other machines are quiet. The surfaces of the cream and white washing machines and driers are chipped, scratched and discoloured enamel. They give me a reassuring feeling as my eyes move across the worn surfaces. The young woman appears to be an extension of the sewing machine she sits at, as she's in a shaded area of the room. Light comes in from the open door opposite me. It cuts a shaft of sunlight across the room, dividing it diagonally, a pleasing symmetry. I feel suspended there with the woman. I know her name. It is Jesse. But for the moment I want to think of her as the woman sewing, an abstract, a shape, which embodies something for me and moves me. There is also something deadening, something of the pall of death in beautiful inanimate objects, or the sight of a pretty woman if I can allow myself to see through the surface. The inanimate coupled with beauty soothes me but also threatens to call me into deadly blissful inertia.

Thus I feel as much of a humming fragile contentment as is humanly possible with the scene in front of me, and I know I could hold it there for as long as I want. And the absorption of the woman, the reassuring ageing of the surfaces, the slightly moving dappled light does start to give me a feeling of deepening comfort as if I were in the most comfortable bed. I'm still in touch with some other part of my mind with all the anxieties surrounding the production that is being pieced together below me. I feel a sickening tension when I allow myself to think about the plays, my plays. I let the queasiness take hold for a while until it gives way and instead I feel my breathing rise and fall in a satisfying way and imagine myself breathing with the woman sewing, both of us caught up in her concentrated stillness, a stillness which seems to flatten the space in front of me into two dimensions.

I am reminded of Max Ernst's painting *Little Machine Constructed by Minimax Dadamax in Person*. His paintings of machines are always anthropomorphic. Life is breathed into the dead and vice versa. Things are both dead and alive, as are we. He does not distinguish between the living and the dead. I find myself seeing Jesse through Ernst's eyes, reorganising her body's template. I know her to be disquieting, indolent, then conversely light-footed. This knowledge of her opens up the possibility of creating an endless number of pared down forms which would represent and transform these parts of her. This process could go much further than painting, or writing, if, in a live performance, the young woman is stripped to her bare essentials by ageing, her sagging flesh implying weakness and worn sinews, and allowed to utter what is barely explicable in a play.

The striking young woman in front of me, Jesse, is the wardrobe mistress. She defies me by looking extremely healthy. Who the hell is she? Well, she makes costumes for the plays and maintains them. But her presence, kindly lent to me in this moment, has taken on a potential for abstraction and generalisation. This is her domain. This is her room and her place of work, but these specifics no longer matter as I'm seeing a portrait of her, beginning to construct a version of her that barely acknowledges who and what she is but can use a line of this and a stroke of that to suggest an embodied internal life.

Once I have my sketch of Jesse formed in my mind I immediately think of my mother and the contents of her room. I must have inadvertently slipped into her body warmth. She has been dead a long time now. The further the distance, the more I have been able to imagine a warmth unsullied by her actual presence, a warmth that barely existed. She was often the vessel of dark rages. And we fought, God how we battled. Goodness, bury her poor soul. I find myself speaking to her as if she could still hear me somewhere.

I was the focus of your fierce loving. I was the one you saw as yours, unlike my brother, who was seen to be more part of my father. I was to succeed you, but you could not have been more mistaken, because I couldn't desire what you desired; your wishes were in turns so concrete, undefined and all-encompassing that they terrified me. I felt oppressed and despairing at your controlling presence. On the surface you worshipped me and wanted to mould me, but really you did not worship me, but thought you saw a projection of yourself. Often, once my actual feelings became apparent, you could not even like me. Your deep love was full of contradictions. How was I supposed to make sense of such opposites?

Yet my father could like me. He just accepted me as his boy, a different boy from my brother. He liked his two clever, physically able, good-looking sons, as he saw himself as a man with a reasonable brain and a strong physical body. What else did his sons need? When my father died I felt the fragile structure of myself fracture. I found the nearest pub. Sitting there with a pint, I knew I needed help. I was thankful to have a friend – friends – to take hold of me then.

I abandon this one-way conversation. I don't like this whining voice, which comes from my mother and is not one that I would like to think as recognisably my own. I'm struck by the thought that George might see me as wanting to dominate him as my mother dominated me, but nothing could be further from the truth. I didn't want to be fucking with him, I wanted to direct him in the play. I was to be his best guide but he didn't accept this.

I yearned for my mother, only to be met with her wanting me to be an extension of her. I had to keep myself separate from her emotional avarice. Edna, my first love, felt just as devouring. So I learned to lust and yearn for her in her absence. This could, out of cruel necessity, set the distance needed for me to feel inviolate. My whole life has been a quest to maintain a sense of being free of intrusion. Silent contact is best, so I have cherished my long companionship with my wife. With her it has been possible to be close to a woman and only exchange the minimum necessary. That is real conversation – not endless chattering. It used to be the same for sex; contact that arose out of absence, hence as a young man I used the brothel houses. With women cared for or loved, when the pressure to perform was unavoidable, the whisky would help, or hinder. Perhaps George thought I wanted to take him over like an obsessed lover – nothing could be further from the truth. It's impossible for me to help George. I cannot offer any actor help in this situation. The crisis is not big enough to talk of radical steps. We can only keep within the frame of the work.

I needed help once. I was falling apart and couldn't face my own sufferings, hypersensitive to all kinds of misery and affliction, large and small. I was given enough to help me understand myself and the implication of others' suffering; that it exists and has to be faced and incorporated into oneself. My friend the psychiatrist helped me by taking me to Bedlam. I shall never forget a young psychotic man, overly attracted to his mother, who reminded me of myself and my own troubles. I was so relieved that the permanent psychotic suffering was not my own, and I learnt that there was a divide between psychological struggle and psychological collapse. The decisive factor at that time for me was to be open to another. It was not without a fight. I gave my shrink a little of my hell. I was angry, insistent in my own superior view, able to show my superior intellect and feel I was at least as clever if not more so than him. I was able to be as ambivalent, ambiguous and as obstructive as possible while also wanting to befriend him. I wanted to show my kind, avuncular man I could understand his analysis as well as him. I had to be alongside him, not just his patient. I could be pretty unpleasant to him and vent my frustration on him. I'd complain about him to my friends. I took his learning for my own purposes. He would have approved: After all, a creative theft is a compliment. My two years of studying the Shrinks and being on the couch, and in a parallel combative relationship with Proust, gave me all the psychological insight I needed for my work. I am proud to say my personality came out unscathed from the encounters with the big psychologists. Jung, whom I came across, also helped point the way: not to lament my physical symptoms and my neuroses but to utilise them while learning to forego habit and the illusion of security.

4. The Flydeck

DOUG THE FLYMAN

I hear someone call my name, 'Doug,' and repeat it more urgently, 'Doug'! A voice from the stage, far below, but the voice seems so distant I feel I do not need to answer it. I am sitting high up on the fly deck. In the furthest corner I could find, away from the auditorium and the stage and the door offstage opposite. The door is stage left, on my left hand side facing out to the audience. It is where people are at a crossroads. All the entrances and exits to and from the outside world happen there. Once crossed, you are on the wooden boards, the imaginative frame of the stage. The book I am reading calls it the contact barrier between what we are sure of and what we need to forget, the bland assurance of the day to day and the disruption of dreams. At the moment I see this space in my mind and I shudder. I can't bear to think of being down there. I know there is a perpetual fault existing under the ground, a cracked ley line. It is permanently in unnatural light or plunged into darkness. It is a hub. Every inch of floor and walls, brick and wood, is painted black. The lighting and sound board are built into the fabric of the walls. It's a mass of switches and sliders; red, yellow and green lights flashing. I feel the panel alive in my mind, dominating it, following the pattern of the nerves passing like fractal lightning through my brain. It is a colossal headache.

When the performance is running, Jane the stage manager sits at the board sending messages and instructions to all the different parts of the building. If I were down there I fear I would feel that my own nervous system was pinned to it, splayed out like a cadaver on a dissecting table. I try to distract myself from the fear of this image by telling myself about Jane and others operating the board. They are not emotionally cued into me. They are the people sending messages and instructions to all the different participants in the building; the wardrobe, electrics, front of house, actors, technicians, and stagehands like myself. They are not even here at the moment. They are out for a late breakfast – what Jesse calls brunch – as the set building is finished. They are out to brunch. I am out to brunch. I laugh. What a relief! I breathe slowly and I feel the tight grip of fear lessen.

I will receive cues from this nerve centre during the performance. The lights will glow urgently while I wait in the dark. I am relieved when I start to think about the lighting board as a matrix, a complex brain that is not my brain. All is quiet and still, the nerves resting. I came up here to rest. I have taken two codeine and need to wait until they take effect. I cannot risk taking anything illegal. I don't have the inclination to do so. I am meant to be resting. I am not resting. My nerves are so agitated. I push my back further into the wall, hard into it so I can feel the painful tension in my back, and ease it. I swept the wooden deck and washed it earlier. It feels clean, the environment made more benign by the removal of dust and the gentle rhythm of the broom and the mop.

I go over the mystery of my vision. How long ago? Can it be a year? She stood hovering at the end of the deck. I knew she was not of this world but all the same she looked like flesh and blood to me. She was a Holy Cow, a kind of benign presence, a cross between the demure Virgin Mary and the beautiful Mary Magdalene – a sinner and a saint? an angel? Ridiculous! How could it be? But she was real and sad and the sadness was so deep it filled me with a chilling, biting anxiety – and terror. I felt my body hoist up with shooting pains in my palms and feet and arse, as if shot through with an enema. At first I was terrified, then free and light and happy. I was high in the air, floating above the stage. Then my body started to metamorphosise. Scissor-like knives came out of my mouth and cut me down. Then I was back on the deck quaking with terror and she had gone. I can't remember when it happened. No one said anything, so no one else saw. I read that it was possible to have these experiences if you were clued into your own subconscious. Jung, he did the same. He brought himself into waking dream states and met his own demons. Remy was telling me about him. He said he survived it because he was basically sane. But can I say the same for myself? Perhaps it's all down to the night of the bad acid. I did try to talk to Jesse about it but she just assumed I was talking about a dream. 'Amazing,' she said, 'far out, fantastic, you have such an extraordinary, beautiful mind.' I wonder if she is the one losing her mind? When she utters these words it is like an emotional storm. And then she and I exist entirely separately with no way that I can love, only hate. I am so often isolated and incapable of loving anyone, particularly myself. I am at heart trying to be good, perhaps more than anyone else.

I don't have to move or look to see the space below me. I can easily picture it. At this God-given height it's a designer's miniature creation made three-dimensional by a model maker. The way the stage set is designed, thirty feet below, is sparse, pared down to the walls at each side and the brick wall at the back. The stage is allowed its full capacity for emptiness, huge, the size of a cavernous church hall. Black flats, braced canvases reaching up to me like tall dark trees masking off the sidewalls. If I were down below they would tower above me. From my position up above I see them cut off, truncated, tapering down in a way that makes me dizzy because they seem to disappear into the ground below. I suffer from vertigo and it is triggered when I look down through this dark forest. I am proud when I overcome the sickening feeling it stirs up in the pit of my stomach. I am good at burying anxiety and fear deep down in myself. When I am afraid I cannot think, but feel attacked. No one can look after me then. Sometimes I have courage, but I see that more and more, it soon leaves me.

Everything below will be blacked out when the performance begins. Anticipating the depth of it frightens me. I see it in my mind's eye, a deepening well. I map it out, trying to contain it. The towering back wall, the vast canvas flats, the scratched and marked floor, the door set into a side panel, are all surfaces giving nothing back to me. The only furniture, right in the centre, is an old battered desk and chair. An ancient typewriter and tape recorder sit on it. A small light hangs over the desk, but it is not on at this moment. I long for it to be switched on and imagine myself doing this, which again gives me some relief. It shines like a beacon cutting through the night.

What of the tape recorder? It is battered and filthy, a machine that might belong to a workman, a decorator, scratched and dented and covered in scraps of paint. One of the stage managers took it from the workshop and is using it as a prop. It does not work. When the audience hears the old recordings, they come through the loud speakers. The repetitions and ramblings set me on edge. The stage manager cues the sound box and the waiting sound technician looking at the mark made on the tape in front of him presses the button and plays the recording. Her movement is automatic and deliberate, mindless, purposeful and fluid. The voice of the recording is eerie, haunting. It echoes strangely in these heights and resonates with the conversations I am having in my head. I had always felt the voices were mine, but lately they seem to be coming from another place. This unsettles me. I feel my nerves start to fire off again and my body is jangling. It is not so much that I am losing my mind as seeming to gain someone else's. I feel overcrowded with shards of experience, each piece threatening to cut deeper into me.

I try to shake this off by coming back to exploring the space below me. It dwarfs me as I stand stationed above it. I'm over six foot, one of the taller men. We are all miniaturised as we drift around on this deck. In my mind I stand up, as if to make a point of my height to myself, and look at the square edges, only seen from this position, that mark the end of the solid black paint. I think of Rothko, whom I truly love, and start to see layer upon layer beneath me of black. I, with him, am looking into raw layers of emotion. Viewing the structure of the installation below helps me to stand to a small degree outside the feelings that threaten to overtake me. How many times have I looked over this edge with my companions, each of us in our own world?

I would be much happier if the flies were filled up with the drops and flats needed for the many scenes in a narrative play, a play which has many characters and a complex story and a need for changing scenarios, where the space up here is rammed to the roof with the clutter of all the backdrops and props needed for the changing scenes, filling up the emptiness. I need the business and the responsibility to help me steer clear of my own fragmented thoughts and ragged sanity. How can the others bear these plays? They even enjoy them. They cannot know how they torture me. Sam, the playwright, looks at the unbearable and they, the crew, all laugh at it? They make a joke out of the old man on stage – they are a bit more in awe of the old woman in *Not I*. But I can't laugh. I can only feel a deepening sense of gathering despair. Krapp is demanding that I care for him and his dilemmas. If I can stand him, will some other meaning be revealed to me? But I cannot stand him! He does not care about anyone but himself. He has lost my goodwill. Can't he, Sam, give me another character, not one whose fragments tax me so much? The whole thing is just a clever display of poetic muscle and style, giving intellectual weight to misery. And George, that beautiful big man, so alive, so funny, all I would like to be, is being destroyed by Krapp. Taken over and diminished. I want to warn him. To tell him to get away. I need to escape and so does George.

Both short plays are also pared down to the barest essentials. In each one, a single figure is centre stage, isolated, cut off from the world, and it seems to me that they are going mad, like me. Am I going mad? I feel a growing identity with the solitary actors, first the woman, then the man. The spaces in the two plays both comfort me and terrify me in equal measure. I am tending to swing from one extreme to the other. I take comfort in the presence of the witness in the first play who stands below the woman as if he is trying to take away the loneliness, absorbing her words into his massive bulk and stillness. Only the woman's mouth is visible and out of it spills her guts. When they did it earlier her entrails came out in a molecular configuration of words, a visceral material substance full of pain, a thick ectoplasm that entered my organs, twisting my stomach into knots. I don't know how I will be able to listen to her night after night. If I can distance myself, even a little... I, too, am transfixed when I hear, no, *see* the words tumbling out of her. There are moments when they are a soothing confirmation of my own pain: I, too, feel articulated, recognised and somehow held in by the witness. I, too, could be made available to another living presence, another mind. But it is more likely that a solid piece of fear comes into me like a poisonous substance flooding my body, burning and torturing my insides. He has no way to digest and report on the outpouring. He is as fucked up as me. I remember a story about a Fellini film. A man is found wandering the streets in Rome. He seems lost and distracted, a lunatic. When asked what the matter is, all he can say, barely audibly is 'La Strada, La Strada,' over and over again. I will be found rolling in the aisles, frothing at the mouth, muttering the titles of the plays, or the odd quoted sentence, making no sense. I am not hugely amused by my joke, but am glad I am continuing the attempt to produce a bit of humour for myself. It keeps up the possibility of a lighter frame of mind.

5. The Theatre Stalls

VIRGINIA THE DESIGNER

Looking at the stage I can see that all is in place, ready for the lighting, a big task for the afternoon. Despite all that is unsettled, I can continue to try to enjoy this last stage, the day of the technical rehearsal and the dress rehearsal. All has moved towards this and the performance tonight. I entered this world of painstaking preparation, the gradual preparation of the maker, when I was a young woman studying with a Cubist painter in Paris. His type of French artists' private school was one of intimate concentration. No one could get lost or hide. If you weren't serious about painting you would not be able to stay there. I went on to an art school in London where, similarly, only the most dedicated and talented were accepted. In Paris and the Slade I would find a world of work entirely my own. It waited for me and I found it. A world where work is all and all is work: the life of a nineteenth or twentieth century painter. Much would be lost without it. I could lose myself in it, and David and I did this together.

I had always loved going to the theatre to see my father's plays. Play readings, when all was beginning, and the energy of the company geared to what lay ahead, were my favourites. I have always loved the opportunity to glimpse the workings backstage.

So it was quite a natural move to take up stage design after college with Clary, who was introduced to me through my father. Clary and her sister and a third woman, all extremely talented designers, ran a stage school and I joined it. My David was also part of it and he eventually married the beautiful, talented Clary. She was both an extraordinarily practical artist and a woman who could make and wear, and eventually manufacture, her own couture clothes – just like Sam's wife. I learned every aspect of theatre there. I had to make props, design sets, act, stage-manage. It was old-style training taken from the repertory theatres where apprentices learn every aspect of the staging of a play by doing productions in rapid turnaround. I have found I always work well with directors who have had some experience of this system. They were often men who had been actors first of all. They, like me, learned theatre as a way of life. This was how I lived for five years, and I would not and I could not have been happier.

When the war came, places quickly shut down and I found myself at the end of the period of training with no obvious place to go. I had met a contemporary of David's, who would become my husband. There was no doubt that if you married and found yourself pregnant, you had found another career. I was still in touch with David and his wife Clary and all that went on in the theatre. Basically, life on the stage continued for those who went to the States. Those who stayed, got on with war work, or one's own work if it served that purpose.

I slipped into an extremely different world, one at odds with the part of me that needed to make things with others, but I hope I made as good a job as I possibly could of being a wife and mother. I embraced marriage with complete surrender and I did the best I could. But ten years later, as soon as David offered me a chance of a job I went back without hesitation, as if I had never left. I was back, my painting gear on, making props and painting scenery.

I soon had a chance to see how simplicity in design could be achieved by eschewing overladen realism, that nonsense that existed then: interiors, tilting rooms, all that palaver. A German company from Berlin had sent a set which I had to copy from sketches and plans that arrived in the post. He gave me a chance to build an abstract concept using another person's design. After this liberating experiment it seemed natural to start doing similar things myself. When I was given my first chance to design something of my own, I opted for two chairs and two doors and a round cyclorama, and I wanted the colour to be suggestive of mood. I painted day and night to complete it. When it came to the time to erect it onstage the technicians were curious, but in a laughing, joking, cool way. I was determined not to let them rile me or get in the way of the concentration needed at a critical moment. When the pieces were sitting on stage before being assembled they looked like a pile of rubbish, ready to be taken away. Gradually the different segments were moved into place. The flats were braced and anchored and looked right. I was pleased and relieved to see them standing up for themselves and no longer bothered with the people around me. David appeared at that moment and confirmed my feelings. The attitude of the young men and women seemed to change when I found my own certainty.

'This is the kind of theatre we want,' somebody said.

I carried out my duties as a mother with a certain amount of paid help. I felt that I did as much as possible to see my children had what they needed, while I had what I needed. But I realise now they were too young and it was hard to lose your mother to another love – the theatre. How many hearts have been broken for a love that cannot be beaten or challenged? Heartbreaking for a child. I always had my mother at home. I did not know how it might feel to be without her. I can see that children may not like their mothers to be passionate about something other than them. It is unfair that it happens. They shouldn't have been hurt, because my desire was not against them. But how could they be expected to understand this? That it is simply a particular sensibility, a type of person, personality if you like, and this person's activities can only be realised through dedication and time. It's a very straightforward equation. Good creative work equals time. They cannot be separated. Had I not given my time to it, I could not have done it. I had to do it. It had got into my blood as a young person and never gone away.

I tried to involve my children as much as I could, thinking they would enjoy painting scenery in the holidays. When they were young, it was a novelty. But that didn't last, of course. They came to resent and dislike it, which was the very opposite effect I'd hoped for. So it was inevitable that I would have less to do with them. David and I worked together day and night. It was the most certain thing in the world that we should have become lovers. We could not be together much, other than working, so much of our feeling was put into letters. David's daughter found some of the letters and the affair was exposed in a painful way.

I felt sorry for both our spouses. It could not be helped. It was fated. Our houses were so close together and there was much wailing and anger and accusation. Both David and I were implacable, which initially riled but gradually smoothed the way. We acted decisively and found studios in Chelsea. I then had the ten happiest years of my life. We worked in tandem. He was the senior Professor and I was the Dean, according to one friend. Extremely clever writers and directors came to join us.

The open invitation to come and make things work, opened doors in many talented hearts and the work sang. David died suddenly in his early fifties. It still seems incredible that that could be so. Why him of all people? He still had so much to offer. Yet he had often alluded to the fact that he had no one to take his place and felt an enormous pressure to continue. His gift to encourage people to be their best on their own terms produced enormous success. People who had cut their teeth with David were asked to come to the new National Theatre companies and David had to keep the writing theatre alive. Did it demand too much of him? He gave it everything. So did I. His death was terrible and I have lived so far beyond him. I simply pushed myself further into my work. I buried my grief in it year after year. I did not speak about it. I did not speak about him. I had my short, blissful happiness, and after that it was complete absorption in the problems that we had solved together.

I kept alive for myself and you. I think you will see that I have not deserted any part of you. Today we are missing your magic and need you to appear in some guise to get us out of an unfortunate hole. Excuse me if I indulge myself and talk to you a little about myself.

'Virginia, sorry to interrupt you, but Anna has asked you to come and see her, is that OK?'

It's Jane with a summons I was expecting. Anna has already confided in me that she is not sleeping. Her child's illness and the play are exacting a huge toll. I follow her immediately.

'Is she in her dressing room?' I ask.

'Yes,' Jane replies.

6. The Theatre Wardrobe

SAM THE PLAYWRIGHT

Earlier, Jesse had put a box of buttons on the arm of my chair and I rouse myself and get caught up, enchanted by its contents. I must be getting senile. But here they are, unexpected riches, banal treasures, prompting. They are an old collection. Brought together over many theatrical years. They seem as old as the rocks, stones and pebbles of my boyhood, and equally alive. When I was very young I did not distinguish between animate and inanimate objects. Everything was vital, spirited, breathing – alarmingly so. I would gather stones to look after them and find safe places to put them in flowerbeds and in trees. Now it seems these old remnants of timeworn costumes are equally alive even though they seem to have been cast off years ago, first out of a far off forsaken factory, then a forgotten performance. They are all sizes and shapes. It was not only that they're different colours; a single one could contain any number of colours as I move it between my fingers and let it catch the light. Each one contains its own character and integrity, whole and indivisible, distinct. I am surprised, absurdly and childishly disappointed when I found ones that match. The fact of one being identical to another flies in the face of my fascination with their difference, and how difference defines and separates one object, one instance, one mark of time and one person from another. They represent the essential aspects of someone, some character, so singular and yet so much like anyone else. The uniqueness is repeated and they are – the same.

There was one button that I particularly liked. It's white with a pearl surface. Held up in the shaft of light it exposes more of its iridescence. I felt I could have turned it endlessly in the light for it held all similar moments. It spoke to me of all my colourful, shimmering instants of feeling, and I could hold it tightly in my hand. Don't mistake me, it is for others to think of the sea on the west coast of Ireland or a bay suffused with light, to think of Bonnard's sweet papers in his studio pinned to the wall. He was an artist who thought he could collect these moments together, whereas I see them as rarer, a distraction, like this button. They're essential to store somewhere, those warmer colours for the more pervasive less colourful expanse of time. A good bottle of wine or conversation will do just as well. But don't overplay it or over-emphasise its value. Variants of black, grey and white tonality are equally fascinating. There are a reassuring number of black opaque buttons in the box. Colour is more like moments of humour, which come out of the darker fabric. Years ago some idiot said to me, 'It's a bright day – will cheer you up.' Completely off the mark. He had the audacity to crash in on my feelings. The light can rise but only when you stay in the dark for as long as needed, when it bottoms out and you find yourself coming up to find the light. Waves of rapture while in the depths of despair bring the good and bad together inside myself and I find myself whole. This is the pathway. Not to obliterate the drabness by intolerable brightness but to hold onto its grounding.

I remember another of Ernst's paintings, *The Forest*, but can see it only in black and white. I know that Ernst's most vivid memories of his childhood were of enchantment and terror. The first time that Ernst could constellate this childhood feeling into an image was when his father led him into the forest near his home. I longed to see all of the paintings, not only *The Forest*, but other Forests, Visions, Suns and Nights. In *The Forest*, human outlines rise out of dark organic tree masses, penetrated by rays of light and star and sun shapes. I can see my pearl button, a spark imposed on the painting I am imagining of Jesse – Frottage, demonstrating an affinity with Ernst.

Still floating in this sea of images I started to look at the holes in the buttons. Why sometimes two and sometimes four? It didn't seem to have anything to do with size. A random decision? – machine-like? mimicking a mysterious accident? aping a systematic mark of meaning? I spot another unusual, small button, brown with a floral pattern and covered with a varnish. I again think of Jesse with unexpected kindness. If I were to paint her I could impose this pattern somewhere. Perhaps I could make it part of the background and make a square of it to one side of her head, in the distorted rectangle to her left. But I would want to place her head in front of it. But then I would black it out, obliterating the reference and pushing it out in favour of other layers. What of the baby she is carrying? How would I convey the tragedy to come? To be born is to arrive in hell and not know it, to be ignorant of the fact that you will die and not know when. That ignorance is the most terrible aspect of a childhood and of those who never come to that reckoning. Those who never give a thought to mortality are the most distorted by it.

I was present many years ago at a psychology lecture given by Jung himself. He talked of a young girl who had no capacity for ordinary feelings; a ten year old, but whose dreams and waking hours were full of mythical images and forms, of which she could have had no previous experience. Remarkable to think of this even now. According to Jung she seemed to be stuck in a collective unconscious and could not comprehend the world of joy and pain. He said that in this sense she had never been born. This struck me as unutterably sad and thoughts of her have remained with me throughout my life. Jung also helped me to understand that my own complexes, all my complicated senses of myself and others would give rise to my own necessary characters. This is how my characters would be given their own legitimate life. Krapp is my most important character in that so much of me is visible through him. And I have not been able to rescue myself from absurdity in this production.

7. The Flydeck

DOUG THE FLYMAN

There has been nothing to do up here for hours. No one else has been up here. All the focus is on the preparations down below on stage and backstage in the wardrobe. I try to doze off but feel too jumpy and wakeful. I should perhaps go out into the square and the sunlight, but I do not want to meet up with anyone. If I met Jane she would want to talk about James. I can't bear how unhappy she is. James has now taken up with Mandy. Mandy really is a whore! She pimps herself. She infuriates me. She thinks it will make me jealous; so pathetic, hurting someone else and not having any idea of the damage she is doing. She is right, the situation shames and hurts me. I cannot do what she wants. I cannot be with her. I am now with Jesse. She does not really want me but she wants to injure me. I want to talk to others but they would only intrude. I could only respect another's view at the moment if it could have some bearing on my own position. I am facing up to what is happening to me and I don't think another person could meet me here.

If I meet any of the others they will want me to join them, and the proximity could push me over into something I cannot control and they would see there is something amiss. If I see Jesse she will attach herself to me when she sees I am not working. I can't stand to be with her when I'm so raw, so bleak. If she gets under my skin I could crack even harder. When we are close, I am mostly preoccupied with the tremendous difficulty of mutual understanding. Sex is the only clear answer. People can be interesting, absorbing, but soon start to disappoint. I know they could never understand what I am experiencing. I simply cannot risk putting myself forward for enquiry. I feel I know more than my contemporaries and I cannot risk exposure to them. They cannot understand me better than I understand myself.

If I were to bump into Virginia or the director they might want to talk about the show. Of course they would want to be discussing something technical, but I do have my own responses and I know they would listen to them politely. But I have no other strong opinion than my fear of the plays, something I could not raise without creating embarrassment and surprise. I fear I could say something that devastates my precarious equilibrium. It may tip the balance. I can only think of myself. I am a coward, which is also despicable.

Something is badly wrong. I sense the tension between George, Sam and the others. It reeks of bad karma. I can see that the words are sacred, each one like Hardy's *Darkling Thrush*. But they are fixed inexorably on death, in sure movement toward extinction... It stinks of empty holes, which suck out any hope I might get from the beauty of the words and the silences. Krapp's voice mingles with mine and drowns it completely. It feeds into my panic. I don't think Jesse, or Mandy, or anyone can see it, Jesse thinks it is exciting and romantic – love of a woman – two women – are mentioned. Jesse's mind is as shallow as a bright puddle at times: a bright clear hollow surface. If I felt mean, I'd say a pool of piss. Miss Piss. She does not see the ice in the words of cold heaven. I see the ice, and it blinds and pierces. I am afraid of the plays, not uplifted by them. My eyes are wide open and I see the horror of the cold expanse where there is no comfort.

I really do feel too vulnerable and need to keep myself quiet. I am trying to empty myself. As soon as a space opens up inside me it starts to resonate with the space around me, which at present feels too black – too dark and empty. A sharp feeling of sadness rises up in me to meet this and drives back the tears, far down into the darkness inside, deep enough, where I can no longer feel them. I stare at a massive knot in the tie rope wound around a cleat and feel waves of anguish passing through me for an unbearably long time. I focus them into the knot. Suddenly I am steady and can think about something else.

I had a moment of shock when I saw Ted earlier in the week. We had been so close at art school. Why had we lost touch? I did not feel ashamed about my job but I could see he was puzzled. 'Are you still painting?' He asked it straight out. I had to say no. And anyway it felt good to be working. I like manual work, I told him. I am a good flyman, conscientious and reliable. I almost said how I felt that it is an important position, I am the guardian of all that is below me, but I held back. He wouldn't understand that. I do feel that is an important post. I need it. I have others' well-being – their lives and safety – in my hands. I have to be cautious and think of others and protect them. It feels good to be seen as strong and trustworthy. I feel the same way with my child. This is all that matters to me, keeping her and myself well guarded. If only I could hold onto her with more certainty in my head. I could see that Ted was disappointed. I felt I had let him down. All these obligations: I want to do right by everyone, but it seems endless. The responsibility stretches out for miles and miles, never ending. I could not talk to him about this, and even less the possibility that I have a new responsibility to save George and Anna from the devastation of the plays. How am I going to do this when I am so afraid? I want to be a good man and to do my duty, but somehow the feeling easily turns into resentment and I resented Ted making me feel bad. Ted and his wife are actively pursuing art careers. I have no interest in this at all. Where has all the passion and interest gone that I had at art school? Or did I? I may have just been doing the same as others around me, going through the motions. Each day I start up with a new hope. Then the next day I experience the disappointment of what had not been possible, and it is an enormous loss, like a death. I then stoke up my desire the following day and feel the next loss and so on, day after day.

Ted's wife had had a drink and she started on me. Why was I not doing more? I was wasting my talent. Ted wanted me to be pleased for his success and to take from his example. But how can my hunger be sated by watching someone else eating? She said I had never been serious. Never worked hard every day. How dare she say what was true? Her speaking it out like that nailed me to the ground. I experience the plays in the same way. I hate them. I hated her. I wanted to hurt her back. 'I have a wife and child to look after,' I said. I could have said I have a girlfriend, too, and another baby on the way. She and Ted have two children. 'It wasn't as simple as that,' they said, almost in unison. But it is! I have never allowed myself enough space. I have always felt full of obligations, to my mother, yes to her. I feel a terrible stab of pain and want to be rid of the image of her. I wanted to shout 'I dabbled and I got through.' An overwhelming despair at the shameful emptiness is always hovering and it is back with me now, as I recall meeting them.

Comfort comes back again from the wood, brick and rope that surround me. I stare harder and harder at them until I feel back in control, master of all that is directly in front of me, master of the care demanded of me. I feel pleasure at the sight of the simple kinetic structures above me, pulleys, ropes, metal bars. There is power that comes with the essential cues performed with concentration and a sure hand. Once the performances start I am in my place, a cog in the inevitable, essential time of the play. Usually I can again find a short period of peace that I experience nowhere else. But there is so little to do, and there is the knowledge of pain and a possible disaster.

TOWARDS LUNCH

8. The Theatre Wardrobe

SAM THE PLAYWRIGHT

I turned to look at Jesse more closely, but a large woman's body obscures her. Janet the wardrobe supervisor has returned from her shopping. She walks bent forward partly because she had been climbing the stairs and has come through the door on the left – stage right – I stand self-corrected. Her figure is clad in black leggings and flowing black and grey robes, large chains of costume jewellery around her neck. I do not see her feet, only her legs and torso and the cigarette in her hand. But I know about her high heels, also part of her tipping forward, and her magnificent untidy crown, an abundance of fair hair. Her arms are full of bags, including her large handbag. She is talking to the designer who comes in fast behind her. Her voice is melodic, and explanations to her companion come out in long vowels, which are picked up behind her. She is a magnificent specimen, physically my type.

The designer has a markedly different entrance, another presence entirely. She is a mature woman in her forties with a beautiful, sharp, intelligent, angular face and thick, dark, untidy hair clipped up behind her head. Her body is spare, bony even. She is my old friend, Virginia. I knew her and her now dead lover, once the director of the theatre, for many years. I love Virginia and feel an instance of joy when I see her arriving. This is perhaps why I am here in the wardrobe. I need to be near Virginia. I know her. I know details of her life (far less interesting than her presence) gleaned over many years. I am amazed as I see her that this knowledge seems completely held in a fraction of a second. It is all of a piece as I apprehend her in the moment of her entry into the room. The other two women, whom I have recently met, are only available in outline. Because of this I feel I can see them more clearly, with less clutter, something plainly essential in their nature. With Virginia I feel a kinship. I cannot separate myself from her. I feel a certain relief in both possibilities.

As the two women enter, the room opens up in front of them, as if the lighting has been increased a few degrees and is subtly flooding the setting, slightly bleaching it. The women don't acknowledge my presence. I'm sitting where they left me earlier. They take me for granted. They adore me and I allow myself to enjoy this, even revel in it. I feel safe with them but I never felt safe with Mother. She abhorred my innocence and sickly disposition. I'm quickly and momentarily back in a place where I'm not yet eight years old, full of the repulsive mix of painful longing and pleasure.

I love to listen to the ebb and flow as the women converse, but I am relieved not to speak. I sit up slightly and the room strikes me differently. I know that it is square but it looks more like another distorted rectangle, which juts out above the building. I know the building is there below me but it is something I am not entirely convinced of, as I'm still able to hang onto a more dreamlike state. In a dream space the room would be detached in some way and an uncertainty would arise about the possibility of finding the building below, the dressing rooms, the toilets, the stairway leading to the stage. All seems remote, cut off from the present moment. I'm glad to be cut off in this way. Not that I can forget about what's downstairs, nor would I want to. Nothing's lost, only a heavily pregnant parallel. It could weigh heavily on me, but I am not resisting it, so it's bearable.

The rectangle splays out further between the three doors, the entrance, the fire exit, the door leading to the wardrobe supervisor's office behind me. The bodies move with the ease of biological clockwork. Purposeful rhythms in tune with the tasks of a workday move in front of me and around me like micro plays; at any moment dialogues and groupings can shift in axis and emphasis.

Virginia sits down opposite Jesse and is bending towards her slightly as she picks through the pile of sample materials that Janet had just placed before her. As her head comes up she is now facing Jesse, who sits at the sewing machine. Something catches Virginia's eye. She looks sharply at Jesse. Jesse comes into sharp focus, and I take in more detail. She is dressed in the hippy fashions of the day, a long skirt and fitted jacket made out of scraps of fabric. Only the slightest swelling at her waist hints at a growing presence. High-strapped sandals on her feet are tucked under the sewing machine. The garment on the machine is a dark colour, mainly black and a line of red sewing is clearly visible.

'Stop,' says Virginia.

Jesse looks up, surprised.

'Let me look,' Virginia says.

Jesse lifts the foot and snips the thread before handing her the shirt she is altering. Virginia looks in angry dismay at the line of red.

'Why don't you change the bobbin? This is a black garment.'

'It won't show,' Jesse says quickly, 'inside the French seam.'

'It's a black garment,' repeats Virginia.

'It saves time, no one will see it, or know that it's there,' says Jesse with some strength.

'I will know it's there,' says Virginia.

Jesse takes back the garment and examines it for a while. She then continues sewing using the red thread. For me her attitude does not suggest defiance but a kind of apologetic movement, showing that she acknowledges Virginia's feelings but the pressure of work means she does not have to give in to her. She seems to say, as she finishes the line of sewing at an assured speed, that Virginia may be her boss and a famous designer, but she is the wardrobe mistress and it is the technical rehearsal, and costumes need finishing as soon as possible. The machine stops. She leans forward and bites the thread releasing the garment. The red line of sewing is a long gash right across the garment. Jesse leaves it on the chair and ignores its reproach as she sets up the machine to fill a bobbin with black thread. The machine is on full power as the thread whirls from spool to bobbin. The noise adds to the drama and tension. Jesse turns the seam inside out and finishes it with a black line. Once she has finished the new seam, the garment is folded and put in one of the piles of costumes to be distributed. Jesse pulls back the garment and looks at it again. With a sharp movement she picks it up and begins to distress it with a piece of sandpaper wrapped around a wooden block. It slips and grazes her knuckles; a drop or two of blood appears. She sucks then looks at her damaged hand, gives up on the garment with a sigh and puts it back on one of the two growing piles of costumes and the stage hands' work clothes, their *blacks*, on the work surface. She and the other two women continue to work and fret and concentrate, Virginia with her notebook and Janet in her office, while I, too, get on with my work. My work is to do nothing.

I sympathise with Virginia. Really, Jesse has no instinct for this drive for detail. But I also sympathise with Jesse, as she will feel the gap in herself in the slight. The garment sits in the pile hiding the failure and I feel an affinity with the way its presence and its hidden garish thread suggest a laceration, a deep history of inner wounding.

Virginia, Jesse and Janet, each one caught up in their own separate, endless, bottomless space. I can hear Janet phoning and organising deliveries, pacing and shuffling in her anteroom. I cannot see her but I know that she moves around rapidly and clumsily, ready to tip over in her high heels. A lot of noisy movement comes from her room; drawers and reference books pulled this way and that. The sound of the soft shuffle of piles of paper being rifled through: pro-formas, invoices, drawings, notebooks, sketchbooks, pens, pencils. These and more personal items are also part of the contents of the huge handbag. I wish I could spend time searching through that handbag just as I had the button box; it would be like putting one's hands into that compact body of hers. Not that I want to get into any of that visceral nonsense – not bodily fluids, no thank you – only to rummage through the extraordinary contents. Contents, which she feels contain her identity – the remnants of a soul. There is a change in tempo as there is a slight clatter of cups?

in trays? out trays? jewellery? Then the unmistakeable sound of a match and the lighting of another cigarette. Janet smokes through the day and evening, as do the people coming and going.

In any weather the young company come through the room to smoke on the metal fire escape outside. The space expands and contracts as people come and go to take a break or to check details with one or other of the women. Virginia has the most visitors as people come to update her on the progress of the set-building downstairs, to ask her advice, or to come to ask her to oversee the placing of something. I withdraw into myself as the space becomes less intimate, busier. An assortment of chippies, electricians, stage managers; the director's assistants are all young and dressed in a mixture of bright clothes and jewellery. I would like them to be all in black, and during the performance many of them will be. The density of light behind the moving masses means that I can, at points, see them as silhouettes, outlines of forms busy on my behalf. I feel like the principle bee with all these workers taking my work on, furthering it, the theatre a hive and this one of its cells. The body masses towering above me are Ernst's anthropomorphic forest trees, all essential growth, arms, legs and teeth. As they throng together (the dark rightly dominating), their combined kinetic energies and the light that breaks through their active shapes create the balance reached in the painting.

Ernst's painting of slightly suppressed horror mixed with edgy, blissful bursts speaks to me of my own formative experiences. All that presses on me visually takes on a surreal quality. I look outwards and the handle of the sewing machine catches my eye, the empty space around it gives it a hard, black, organic form. It frightens me. The shape that emerges is so distinct and unusual; my insides actually turn over and sway, struck by a powerful otherness. I look again at the thing that has lost its functional shape and an image of black water comes instead.

A dark presence has jumped out of the visual field and I am swimming in the Irish Sea with fathoms of darkness and loneliness below me. What an extraordinary moment and place to start hallucinating. The presence of death slaps me in the face, a huge stinking fish. I steady up, supported by the chair beneath me. I feel I'm ready to deal with this but am not sure where it's coming from. I have learnt to respect the terror of loss. The unavoidable knowledge of death prompts endless variants of psychological dying. I ride with it. No one suspects this is going on. Then it takes another turn. The horrors have an amusing, contrary energy, which works with and against it. A movement occurs as a result of moving away from the terror towards its counterbalance; energy, light and a creative doing – a bit of outlandish humour – 'Oh, we're out of that now.' The problem (and it happens fairly often) is that it is pointless attacking it with the will. I feel tremors now. Luckily, part of me knows that there will be an inevitable, unconscious shift.

9. The Flydeck

DOUG THE FLYMAN

I open my eyes. It is lunchtime? The small door opening onto the roof is ajar. I let myself take in the light and feel the fresh air. It must have been open all the time I have been sitting here. I can see the rooftop, slates, roof tile and brick, grey with the patina of old London smog and grime. I would have to get up and stoop to go through it and stand on the roof. The large roof space outside was full earlier on with all the stagehands sitting there having a cigarette while the endless preparations continued downstairs. We had all come back from breakfast and were just hanging around. People were drinking beer at an early hour, anticipating a long day with little to do, punctuated intense activity. I did not approve of this cavalier attitude and felt myself more allied with the designer and production manager downstairs who were trying to sort out the technical problems. I see myself as an integral part of the production. I am as important as anyone else. I have a place in this unholy synchronicity.

I see myself sitting on the parapet, smoking. I do not much like cigarettes, the acidic bitter taste, but I crave a smoke like everybody else. It fits well with the slight, and not so slight, uncomfortable tensions that come with social contact. Mild anxiety is followed by an instant puff of pure relief provided by the sharp chemical hit of comforting smoke in the lungs. 'Mother's Milk,' says James, and he could be right. I see myself bent forward over my thighs and tight jeans. I imagine myself as others see me, a tall man, well built, a strong back and shoulders covered in a fitting, long-sleeved shirt with an open neck. I am dressed in the same uniform as the others, Anglo-American Cowboy. James is even wearing the boots! The others see me as strong and serious. They are always respectful and treat me with a degree of caution. They fear me in some way. I think it has to do with my size. I see it in the street sometimes. Men back off. Do they see something violent in me? They certainly seem to be pushing their violence into me. How else could I be feeling so angry? This is unfair and absurd, because I would never use my strength to threaten anyone. I can catch myself enjoying it, though. It's a powerful position to be handed on a plate. Why not take some pleasure in it? But the terror pushes me away. I long for people just to see me. What if they found out about the strange, frightening, half-arsed images in my head? I can't talk to anyone about those. All they know is the gossip, the surface, which is to know nothing, nothing about my exquisite suffering. I intend to keep it that way.

I go back to an attempt to enjoy the image of me smoking. What a handsome man, curly black hair and a shapely moustache. When I laugh, they laugh too. I am infectious, urrghh, what disgusting vanity. I can feel close to the men standing there, hanging out, Paul the Australian, Remy and one or two others. The beer they are drinking is left over from the beer Jesse brought over for us yesterday. The discussion goes in familiar circles and there is a fair amount of humorous banter. A group of men standing or sitting against the sky; their young, faultless bodies up against the blue and white of clouds and the black and white marble of weather-blackened, mortar-streaked London brick. We look like Gods. I want to cry. I wish I had my guitar with me. I could play *The House of the Rising Sun* and twist my moustache into a Salvador Dali caricature, put my baseball hat on back to front. It is great to sing clichéd popular songs – The Beatles – with everyone singing along as if life depended on it.

But I would not have the energy now to sing, even if I had the opportunity to play.

Instead I hang around, my mood getting lower and lower. The roof is as desolate a stage as the staging of the play inside. The roof is painterly, masterly brush work, covered in guano. The pigeons hover around carelessly, depositing more of this white noxious fluid during their repetitive, monotonous calling. The colour of the birds' bodies, fluorescent purples and reds against the monotone, make them appear as poisonous as their acidic shit. The thought of eating one is to find my mouth filled with rot and vermin. Their bodies move like ugly, shining maggots against the black and white canvas. Someone attempted to feed the birds, old loaves of bread spilling out of their plastic wrappers are strewn about. The slices of bread, curling and dirty, have turned, in large patches the colour of orange and purple, presumably the result of the chemical additives e Bright Orange and e Bright Purple, in mock facsimile of Vermillion and Pure Windsor Violet. My feelings run in two directions. I feel two opposing instincts, to act on outrage at the contamination of basic commodities, and the urgent need of a canvas and brushes.

As I'm feeling sick, I need to decide to leave off remembering attempts at male camaraderie. I feel a complete failure. I cannot even manage a thin semblance of normality. I exit out of the door backwards, taking with me the memory of the beautiful, heroic, doomed young men against the sky. They resembled a moment of hope, but the noxious atmosphere around them tells another story. I reel from the elements that speak only of death and decay. Life is stacked against me. I stumble across the bridge high up between the two fly decks, and rush down the stairs leading past the dressing rooms. I cannot bear to see anyone and no one crosses my path; a good omen – for them. I relieve myself in the front of house urinal next to the stalls bar. A young man cottaging picks up my vibe and flees. I stand for a while before I turn back to retrace my steps.

10. The Theatre Wardrobe

SAM THE PLAYWRIGHT

I am free until the actors arrive. And here, to my annoyance, they are stopping my reverie, coming one after the other through the door. I have no choice but to respond to the actors' demands for attention. We all have to. They demand what others do not dare. I was never sure about George as a choice for Krapp. How could a famous actor, whose looks and seductive charisma are part of his essential acting equipment, be the everyman at the end of his rope, willing with some equanimity to be poised on the edge of the terror of being a living intelligence? When I met him I'd hoped that slight ageing, from life's vicissitudes, would take him further into himself and he would have a powerful presence and self-deprecating humour, which I felt would come through. It is emphatically not coming through. I was surprised to find that he is actually quite cold. Virginia has said he must be feeling compromised, self-conscious, abandoned even. George needs to feel I am behind him. But who is to blame for that? Not me.

I liked the way George at first gave everything to his task, and did not seem to challenge how the words carry the character. There is no character, only the words! But he will not let me help him inhabit the text. All must inhabit the impact of the musical breath in the sound. It's hard for the actors never to waver from the minute emotional emphases in the constant shifting of tonality and exacting rhythm, and the pauses demanded in the words. If he let himself go back and forward in the sound of the phrases and silences he would have a chance to find the unconscious associations belying the words. I could weep when I see these transformations. It pleases me when the actors don't impose some other inappropriate limited interpretation. I hoped that if George let me instruct him, let me show how the words carry him, then his essential qualities would come through to make it a unique performance. He would experience living through me, the writer, and my character.

George brings weight; the weight of his body and his voice, and his experience. But he would not let me guide him into something that is much bigger than he. He treated me as if I was interfering. That was too much to tolerate: such a distortion of my intentions. George is a King Actor and I want this king to be my king. I need George to be my king to match Anna, who is my Queen, but he doesn't allow me in. George can only change if he changes his position towards me. But he is averse to self-enquiry and it is always the other who has to be at fault. He cannot do this on his own. He thinks he can. He will wait in purgatory as long as he will not work with me. And I have given up on him.

Anna had done many of my plays. I know she can find a way to speak through my words, to trust that I know the import of each syllable. She knows that I am guiding her towards something that she and I can only feel, not know exactly. Famous actors may be unable to play these parts, as the parts demand that they give themselves up. But George cannot focus on an abyss because his life is too soft. It is full of sex and women and glamour. This is a horror and I find it unbearable to be with him. When I was rehearsing with him he kept deferring to Peter, as if he could not stand me.

I suspect he thinks that he knows Krapp as a whole character better that I do. But Krapp is not whole and mapped out like a set on a stage. No, he is like all of us in a movement between being whole and in fragments. George sees my character as a series of dull habits, not as an amalgam of previous countless subjects and Krapp's innumerable individual adaptions to others and himself. He is always in a dangerous zone, a perilous state of mind. He is always in pain but also has mysterious energies and still has a creative, fertile, febrile mind. This means he is aggressive, envious, unpredictable, forever nascent, Jamesian, Proustian, pain itself, his habit of boredom long replaced by active suffering.

The King and Queen stand before the three women and me. They are sovereign to my two kingdoms, two so-called short plays. George is partly dressed in the blackdark- layers of a man's worn-out formal dress, his white shirt sleeves unbuttoned, waiting for Jesse to give him his waistcoat so that Virginia can look at the final effect. His outfit could belong to any class; labourer, clerk or professional, an artist, or a thief or clown. He, George, seems to have little comprehension of how much the black and white costume, finished with his oversized white clownish shoes, means to the play. He is standing there, pulling it around to see if it fits and makes him look compelling. How could I have thought he could play someone who is my age – late sixties? He is meant to be shipwrecked, but no amount of working on him can make him feel the complexity of ageing. The dark and light are like the notes on a piano and all the notes of the play are musical sounds, visual and verbal illusions, nothing is literal. If I felt it would make a difference I might try to articulate this for him but it would not be the right way and I cannot waste any more of my breath on him.

I turn to Anna, who is covered from head to foot in black. There are two slots for eyes but they are barely visible. On stage only her mouth will be visible high up in the proscenium arch. Only her mouth will be lit, and out of it will pour a woman's life in so many anguished fragments. The speed of her uttering will be faster than the speed of thought and the listener will be struck by the emotions and sounds. The words and their literal sense come through spiralling repetitions. The shape of a cloaked figure, the auditor, will cast an attentive shadow below her. Anna stands now, having removed her hood, waiting. I have less doubt about this one. The second of the single-handed plays is a delight to direct, with a delightful, sharp, quick-witted actress who has no pretensions, nor actor's protective airs or armour. But it is a new play and we have a way to go yet. I was frightened by the feelings I sensed in her when she broke down in front of me. Was she disappearing into the shattered realm? Could she really break down and not recover as a result of portraying this? Have I taken it too far?

George takes his coat and puts it on. Jesse fusses over him, smoothing the costume down unnecessarily as if he were wearing a tuxedo. I hold in my irritation. None of it is on the surface. George is not aware of the red thread that runs through the garment like a set of nerves, concealed by the doubling of the seams. The red cotton mimics his own inevitable threads of frustration and anger. He shows none of this as he flirts and jokes with Jesse, getting the attention he expects. I keep silent and he does not meet my eyes. The space now feels its real size, small and crowded.

Anna looks on and waits her turn. She smiles at me discreetly. She knows I love her, platonically but passionately. Who in the company does not know this? I now completely ignore George. Anna does not want to hurt him. She is sensitive to George's position but understandably glad not to be there herself. Not that she would, she is too intelligent an actress for that, eager to meet my demands as her writer and director. We are in complicity, while I have abandoned George to Peter's care. He must in part be relieved, but no actor's self esteem can be untouched by such a rejection. What can I do? I cannot accept what he is doing. I am unsparing with myself. I ask him only what I ask of myself. Peter will never be able to give him what only I can give.

Anna and I begin to talk as George looks on. I feel his presence diminishing and I am relieved. I wish he would just go but he is here for a reason, the costume fitting, and will not go until Virginia says so. Anna's voice soothes me as much as it haunts me on stage. I have nothing but admiration for her. I have so enjoyed being able to go home with her after the rehearsals and go over and over the text in an effort to establish the right orchestration. I did push her too hard and Virginia was right to intervene and to give her a break. I regret that and I did say I was sorry.

'You can imagine what it is like up there in the dark, Sam. They have raised the platform so high – and in the complete dark I am afraid I will tumble. But that is not the worst of it. I am completely shut in and the disorientation is terrifying. I'm not just moving through the script and the pace but also a feeling of falling into a void. I am so sorry, so sorry I broke down earlier.' She looks again on the verge of tears.

' Oh Anna,' I say, and I feel wretched. 'What have I done to you?'

'I know it seemed as if I was saying I wasn't sure how I could return to the rehearsals and go on, but of course I am determined to continue, but how am I to get over the awful fear? I don't know how I can, but I will go on.'

'Of course you will,' I say, 'I never doubt you will go on.'

She looks frightened but also bemused.

Virginia comes in slowly.

'The problem is being solved.... we will strap Anna into a specially built armchair. It's almost complete and will be ready for the dress rehearsal. Her head will be wedged between two blocks to make her feel secure. There will be no chance of falling.'

I'm satisfied. She will get on with her task. I change the subject to someone I know is important to her. 'How's Mary?' I say, remembering her daughter who is ill.

'She is better. She's being well looked after by her father.'

I move on as the subject is settled in my mind, at least she is safe. She has indicated to me that she is fearful for her sanity, but I can only let myself believe that she is strong enough to deal with this.

I hear Anna's melodious voice and am aware of her slight, strong, compact womanly body. She appears to me invincible. We have the same sensibility. There is an unbreakable bond between us. I shall make as many plays as I can for her. She turns to Virginia to allow her to inspect the black garment she is wearing. It will make her body undetectable in the dark. The awful mental discomfort and the alienation felt so deeply in the dark can only enhance the feelings provoked by the play. She has allowed me to orchestrate every single word in the waves of the monologue. I conduct her emotions like the moon and the weather, pulling the directions of the tides. I follow her movement as she follows mine. Anna will find a way to deal with her state. She indicates as much as she turns to Virginia and demands nothing more of me. Her performance at the rehearsal was nothing short of miraculous.

The posters should declare *Two Short Plays – One a Miracle, the Other a Disaster.* The reviews are bound to say just that. I turn to look at both actors. At least in costume they each look their parts. Virginia has done an excellent job as usual. There is nothing to add. Relief is at hand, a call for the lunch break is heard and the actors, satisfied with their costumes at least, leave.

Actors can tolerate being a conduit for both the dark and light forces of human nature but few can take it to extremes. A seasoned or famous actor has learnt to rely on prodigious facility and skills: George has a safety net created by the parameters he has set himself and is not likely to give this up. People who can give themselves to my plays are gifted in that they can take the risk of not understanding, not knowing, fishing in the grim side of human existence and finding its opposite, a lightness, a dazzling. To be aware of the real is to face the terrors of life. To dare to be aware of these facts takes courage. And there are rewards in so doing.

My character, Krapp the writer, has dared to try to bring the forces of mind and body together in his work. We see this in the way that he is now a mix of comic beauty and devastating tragedy, ugliness and beautiful, sparse forms of loneliness and punctilious language. Any artist, such as my character, another writer, religious thinker or psychologist is punished for daring to attempt to bring together this split between lively beauty, murderous ugliness; mind and body, sense and spirit. If he takes these opposites and makes them one, he is liable to be punished. I remember Jung's lectures. He made it clear that there was a powerful internal demand for the mind to be closed off from the intolerable shadow, our real nature, kept safely but lethally concealed like a hidden missile. But if it can be pulled off, if the pessimism can be included and watched, we can feel the amelioration of it.

LUNCHTIME

11. The Theatre Wardrobe

SAM THE PLAYWRIGHT

Sick of myself and waiting, I want to think about images in paintings instead. Paintings I had first seen when they were being made many years before. I knew enough French and learnt more German to enable me to understand them beyond a fanciful, imposed narrative. The exhibition of paintings a few years ago at the Tate had again confirmed this view, developed decades before.

The curator, that big, rich, ruthless woman with a razor-sharp instinct for pictorial language had shown, through her collection, how visual abstract language highlighted the essential elements of all aesthetic relationships.

She exposed me ruthlessly and unfairly in writing when I was still a young man, calling me homosexual because I did not want her. The thought of her huge body still stirs me – not sexually – but she did excite me intellectually. I could find room for a passionate desire for her because she had no place for progeny in that big-boned carcass of hers, only her collected artefacts. Her gifts were but one example of the vast amount of riches given to me by the women in my life. We looked together at modern painting in the twentieth century and saw the mind's capacity to project its own imprint, showing the minimum necessary to see the opposites, the horror of mortality, and life's tantalising unfulfilled promise. I had been satisfied to see how I could bring this alive in my plays. I could give the additional element of language to the visual.

Virginia, too, understood this visual necessity. She emptied the stage of all deadening weight of stuff, outmoded tedious realism, and left it with just the essential elements needed for the characters to emerge unencumbered, letting the inner world emerge. My insides feel evacuated by all this delving into myself. I am beginning to feel a little weary and hungry, and I come out of my reverie to find that the wardrobe has emptied out, Jesse clearing up around her machine.

'I'm off to lunch,' she says. 'Do you want me to bring you anything? I'll be about an hour.' I ask her for a ham sandwich. 'Yes, I'll get that for you. See you later.'

After that it really is quiet. There is no more hum from downstairs and it has become warmer, a slight buzz of insects outside. I really should get out of this armchair, I think. But I don't want to. My grandmother had had a bed in a cupboard in her house, which I loved as a boy. I think again of *The Forest* and wish I had the catalogue here so I could look at it again.

I wake up to a good deal of commotion. There is a clambering and clattering up and down the backstage stairs, voices questioning and calling out. Janet is agitatedly moving around looking behind furniture and under piles of costumes.

'Damn it,' she says, 'my handbag's been stolen. Didn't you see anyone, Sam? Someone got in while we were at lunch. Charlie has lost jewellery and others have lost their bags.'

I'm on my feet telling her I must have fallen asleep. I feel alarmed and strangely guilty about Janet's handbag. Jesse is checking her stuff.

'I had my bag with me. There's nothing of value in mine. Luckily no one would take the costumes. Piles of rags, really.' She looks sheepishly at Virginia.

Virginia attempts to commiserate with Janet. 'What have you lost?' she asks.

'My bag,' says Janet, in some distress. 'It had my keys and chequebook and money and photos and makeup – the whole caboodle. The idea of them and my things.' She bursts into tears. 'Bastards, coming through the window while Sam slept. How am I going to get home?' She weeps harder, while the others awkwardly attempt to console her.

I move into the office where the bag had been left. I do not quite mean to go there but it is the only place I can move into once out of the chair, the room is so full. The police have arrived. I catch sight of myself in the mirror. I am startled. I expect to see a man dressed in a form of black nineteenth century costume, a sort of pared down Dickensian outfit. Instead I am my usual self, wearing my light summer raincoat, light trousers and a white shirt. My hair has been recently cut, as have my nails, and I look very much the fastidious Parisian in contrast to those around me. I recognise my famous figure seen in photographs all over the world. I cannot help but be amused by the absurdity of someone stealing things around me while I sleep in the armchair. No one else is showing any interest in me since discovering that I was unconscious.

I see that the two policemen are looking out of the open window, looking out through a gully to the London square. 'They could have gone down the fire escape, Madam,' one says to Janet, 'but that would have been noisy. They may have worried about being seen and stopped. They might have got in and out over the roof. Is it possible to climb up? Might be worth looking up there. Looks like someone very agile got in, without disturbing someone's sleep?' Jesse puts her head out of the window.

'Looks easy enough to me. I think I could hop up there.' And before anyone has a chance to say anything she has climbed onto the window-sill and disappeared.

Almost immediately we hear her cry, 'I've found it!' Jesse quickly hands Janet's large bag down, delivering it into the hands of one of the policemen. The man opens it and recoils. 'Ugh. It's not very nice, I'm afraid,' he says.

'Let me look,' says Janet, pushing him aside. 'Oh, how disgusting! How could they?' She bursts into tears again, a long howl turning to sobs. Jesse leads her away. At last I will be able to see in the bag. I feel a slight guilt at my own enjoyment of having my wish granted to peer inside, close enough to look into the bag. I feel a wave of revulsion. It still smells strongly. But that is not the whole of it. It was not only the enormous size of the crap but the soiling and spoiling that repulsed me. I'm transfixed until I hear my name being called over the tannoy. I walk out of the room and down the stairs to face the afternoon rehearsals. I do not stop as Jesse calls after me, 'Sam, you've forgotten your sandwich.'

12. The Theatre Stalls

SAM THE PLAYWRIGHT

Ah, the relief of being alone again. In the darkened stalls you can be nicely separated from the rest of the world. I have always had a clear feeling of difference and needing distance from others. It started at school. I realised then that my preoccupations were not in tune with others. But I couldn't share any of that. It bothered me and I did wonder if other boys experienced a sense of a parallel existence. I could inhabit a sort of physical hiatus of extremely variable intensity, which at worse was a sickening feeling in the gut and genitals, ribs sticking to the lungs as they moved in and out; a slight pressure on the body, its skin in a state of surprise, wonder and disbelief at the overwhelming sensations. I felt everything around me as intense waves of physical discomfort, or pleasure. It was not primarily the result of what I saw. I simply absorbed my environment by a process of emotional osmosis, through my pores, skin, hair, testicles, toenails, palms, sweating, hair raising. Later in life these became my symptoms of anxiety and depression; boils in every conceivable crack, depressing septic cysts, palpitations, night sweats, insomnia, and fear of madness and dying.

I was part of a family that valued books and sport, positive attributes of the Protestant middle classes in which I could immerse myself. So to counterbalance my sensitivity I roughed it in sports and play and worked hard at my studies. Furious to find myself so porous and tender, I threw all my raging energy into a ball or a bat – I could throw myself out of a tree or into a river from forty feet or more. There was no end of the physical activity I could hurl myself at. This way I found myself an integrated member of society. The external bashing was much kinder than the internal one. And

I could bash others with my intellect and obvious mental superiority. This was my most reliable retreat from suffering, particularly from my mother's savagery. I could experience her in reverse. Give her a bit of her own disgusting tasting medicine.

My observing skin kept itself alive even though I flayed it on the cricket field, on the rugby pitch, running in the cold dark of early morning, scouring with cold showers, plunging into cold rivers. I staked my hide out in all weathers; wind, sleet, snow and scorching sun. Exhilaration survived the knocks and bruises. Adrenalin and other energies released by exercising and straining the musculature made me feel I could live through anything. Watching sport, I still remember my extraordinary determination to push through the psychological barrier – in and out of contact with myself – no longer apart from the world but pulsating with it. And, as I realised later, still protected – still in my own sphere.

Sexual contact could have the same problematic possibilities. Early romantic sexual contact was better felt as distant – taken into the protective one-ism, where raw emotional contact could be avoided. Coupling was too much of an onslaught for the senses: all the organic, orgasmic squishy roundness, swellings and protuberances. But once I was older, much older, it was possible to key into a slower pace – not thrust about by surging hormones, feelings and physical bits popping upwards and outwards, like allergic rashes. Later, when I could tolerate my own body more, its physicality as well as psychological feelings, I could stay with my own arousal and not find it overwhelming. The physical longing for another became possible with or without romantic yearning. If only this could have been possible with my first love. To have given her a demonstrable love before she died. So young. Who does she remind me of? Now? She reminds me of Jesse. Not that I feel any of this towards Jesse. She is an attractive young woman but far too slight physically and too flimsy intellectually for my taste. I like a woman who is extremely bright and can speak her mind, like my lover and companion, Fay.

When I left school I could isolate myself and undertake less and less. I could wallow in contempt for others and myself. The morbidity of what I was doing did not strike me at the time. I could sneer at others, and the miserable solitude and apathy guaranteed my superiority. It was not until I developed the symptoms that I became aware of something masked and atrophying in myself. I went to Geoffrey, my friend the psychiatrist, and then to Bion and found the symptoms were only the tip of the iceberg, and that my condition lay in my prehistory, with my poor benighted mother. Had it not been for that time in London – and the analysis – would I have continued boozing and lounging and sinking into further disintegration?

13. The Theatre Wardrobe

JESSE THE WARDROBE MISTRESS

Thank goodness people have scattered. I can go into Jenny's office and look where I've hidden the stash. Great, it's still here rolled in the cloth. Of course it's still here! No one was looking for it. I felt quite agitated when the police were here. I thought they might start taking the place apart. Anyway, I'll just take a peak.

I love rolling the cloth out and looking at it. The hashish's sweet pungent smell is so pleasing and repulsive, the smell of an illicit substance. No wonder it's called shit. It's a shame I can't smoke it now that I am pregnant. I can sniff at it instead, enjoying the smell, forgoing the effect. I sit on the floor and make myself comfortable and protected, leaning back with my head under the table. In this child's den it is pleasing to be by myself. It was an inspired idea to make another material store in this gap under the large desk. I can hide under here and no one would think to look for me. What a brilliant idea! I might spend more time here, only if Jenny's not around, of course.

The smell of the heavy fabric adds to the mustiness of the stench of weed, a mixing of soothing, sedating aromas. The last time I smoked I felt frightened, my body alive with the pulsating presence of the weed and the baby, and I was alarmed by this growing responsibility. It felt as if it were the first time that I was in touch with my pregnant self, and an uncertainty arose which I didn't welcome. I need to feel light and able, not overburdened or afraid.

There had been a strange exchange with Roger. He rang to say he'd gone to the house to collect the next batch of stuff. He rang the doorbell and found the house empty. The people had 'blown out' he said. I didn't believe him. I knew he was lying. He never lets anyone get the better of him. He had taken my money, one hundred pounds, for himself. I was surprised because I knew he was capable of it but I didn't think he would do it to me. I don't feel too angry, even though I should feel furious. No, it relieves me of the whole project. I no longer have to sell it. It was easy money, too easy. This suits me. It came to a natural end. A shame about the cash, but money always comes and goes. It will not stop me going to university and having the baby.

I do not want my equilibrium disturbed. I love being pregnant. Thinking of the tiny baby inside me makes me move further back and snuggle into the bales of fabric. I wish I were in bed at home dreaming about the baby. Or holding the hand of my friend Simon's daughter, Rose, crossing at the bottom of Kensington Church Street, where she lives. I am aware that others think she belongs to me. 'She's her child,' is what they are saying to themselves. It's obvious to me from the way they look pleased and satisfied. Pleased by our completeness.

When Simon asked me about the baby, I said without thinking, 'I shan't ever be bored again.' I regretted instantly showing myself up so starkly. As soon as the words came out I wished them back in. It did sound shallow. I am not having the baby because I am bored. Or am I? I should have said, 'I shall be complete,' something like that. I feel delighted, so full up. I now have a purpose. I cannot feel anything other than pleasure. I love the fact of my growing insides. I am surprised when people are not happy for me. I'm not married, I know. But so what? Others see me in a precarious relationship. It is none of their business. They do not see what I see. Doug is the mirror image of me. Our being together is so perfect and inevitable. I really do feel sorry for those who don't feel how delightful it all is.

When I told my mother, I could feel her dismay. I laughed. I was taken by surprise. I reassured her that I was extremely happy, and Doug was with me. That he accepts I am having a child and we are making plans. I am off to university and he is getting a job in the same city. We're going to live geographically closer to my mother, away from London, away, far away from Doug's wife and the vampish Mandy. Hurray for the move! I would like to take the train straight away. The hustle and bustle of it all, I am doing it now in my head. I am powerful, powerfully busy.

My life is going to be full to the brim, pushing out darkness over the cup's rim. I stretch out, exercising my happiness, making it fill every atom. Then I am curled up like a freshly made croissant, deep under the table, and I have metamorphosed into a croissant cat carrying a kitten embryo. The little kitten is tiny and completely grey, with the prettiest face and the liveliest blue eyes. I have images of the baby as all kinds of animals, as well as a human baby. But the image that comes in strongest is Simon's Rose. She is my ideal, so kind to me, angelic, beautiful and gentle. She quietly puts her hand in mine when I arrive at their house. My cat's bed is so warm and cosy. I feel a lump under my head, the drugs are now an irritant, a pea in the princess's bed. I need to stop selling it. I needed the cash but it's too risky. The police could have found it, and what then?

I feel telescoped under the table. I made an Alice in Wonderland costume recently and imagine myself wearing it. It's a light blue cotton dress, the most delicate blue with a slight gauzy sheen. It glows in the light from the window. It is finished with a small white apron, nipped at the waist. The skirt is a pleasing fullness. The idea of it makes me feel girlish and oddly sexy. My mother would say I look extremely fetching. She would be delighted to say it shows off my good legs. I would like to be painted in the costume, a last picture of my young womanhood before I have my baby. It would have to be post-impressionist, as Doug says I should have a full colour range, which would say everything necessary about my essential self.

I am no longer in the Alice in Wonderland dress but in my day clothes under the table. I picture Doug sitting in the flys. I start to feel sexually aroused. Must squash that feeling and remember where I am.

The time I have spent living and working in this theatre takes shape in the room. The piles of materials and reference books, drawers for samples, ledgers of papers, they are the geology of my time here. When I moved into this room it was empty, bare of furniture or cupboards and shelves. The once empty room is now full. Each layer could represent some memory or trace of my experience and what I have learnt. So much evolves in small stretches of time. I have been taken so far beyond the life I had before I came here. As my focus deepens and I pick out each detail, there is something cluttered, random and meaningless and its layered density gets to me. These impressions are better shrugged off. Instead I marvel at the richly patterned pieces of cloth and their texture, a soft woven dark fabric, a raised brocade, and thin delicate cotton, like the dress, in pastel or bright colours. Its brightly coloured mass, a kaleidoscope, enters my consciousness. I will not let the dark or the negative dominate. I can just switch it over. I want to stay here, forever immortalised, somehow captured as a cat-odalisque in a picture.

We all went off together to the Matisse exhibition a week or so ago before the evening performance of the last play. I loved it because Matisse does not have any anxiety or edginess in his paintings. And I loved all the materials in the pictures. He is said to collect pieces of fabric, prized props, which he uses to dress the sets for his portraits of women. I imagine him pulling them out of a huge dressing up trunk. There is nothing but calm and beauty – *Calme, luxe and volute'* – what wonderful words to wrap around the tongue – so unlike the play downstairs with its Carravaggio darkness. God, it's tense down there. And the actors do seem on edge. Particularly George. They are lovely to me, charming and kind as all good actors seem to be. There is so much warmth in a company. The feelings for each other are stronger than other peoples' working experience together. Even if tempers get frayed, the actors and crew usually soon get on again.

Each swatch of material placed round me represents a person, a book, plays, world cinema, new tastes, new foods, alcohol, drugs, hippies and punks, travel and the endless unfolding of the city, a space that can never be encompassed and fully known. The fabric of a city, any street you walk down contains any number of historical remnants. The most important layers contain the moments of my passage through the buildings and streets and my encounters there. They are my own fossil record, which is part of a whole geology, impossible to unearth.

The fabric stands for the building material of the city of London, which is always shifting and forever changing. It is so big and rich it cannot be charted, just like the mind. I would always want to live here, at least in my head, and always need to come back here to this city – this place under the table.

Doug and I have such blissful afternoons off together – extraordinary and weird. Doug and I and a few of the others saw a film by Man Ray of people moving around the Paris streets in the 1890s: most of the people in this film would now be dead. In thirty years' time, none of those people will be alive. The sheer number of people already dead shocked and amazed me. It had the same impact as the news of a massacre. They all looked healthy, strong and attractive, the city seething with life. Whole populations disappear without murder or mayhem; just through the passage of time. I can see their bodies petrified into the buildings around them, their substance having an endless capacity for absorption of matter. Remy said that there is a finite amount of matter in the universe and that it is constantly recycled in some way. Are all populations just fodder for some organic cycle? It all suddenly feels distant and abstract. I have felt that about the plays. I am so taken by them, but the impressive desolation of the characters seems remote when I think about my new life and my baby. If Sam's characters had had children or could love a child, wouldn't their anguish be soothed away?

I imagine the baby dancing inside me, a beautiful, comic dancer, a lovely fair-headed hermaphrodite boy-girl. Maybe he would be like me, bright-eyed, a little too bright-eyed in those early photographs. Could I detect a hint of painful over-activity in my small self? Do I detect it in myself now? An enthusiastic neighbour described me as precocious, able to speak early, and affected by classical music played to me as a three year old. I was a beautiful, sentimental, light blonde-haired child. And the black brightness of my own three year old eyes? I won't linger on it. I can make nothing of it.

I think about my mother who was slim and dark like Picasso's blue woman when she was young. She is still beautiful in her forties but has lost her inner light. What had she been like as a baby? I can't for the moment recall any photographs of her. Photos of me come into my mind instead. But the one with the teddy bear is her, and I look identical to her later on. Already identities are confused, history conflated. Will the baby be a clone of me? I hope not, and I hope so. I remember a photo of a baby in a huge pram. No, that was Dad. A large plump child sits up in a massive Irish Protestant pram with a wave of curly hair, a mini quiff. Again, I feel stabs of pain, a longing for the past to be different. He is such a reclusive, unhappy man, clever but uninterested in other people. Did he already feel isolated and slightly superior sitting in the enormous pram? Everyone looked down on my father, but he certainly did the same to them.

My father always liked babies. My mother told a story about him disappearing after work and her suspecting he was having an affair. One of her friends in the office said that she had seen him in deep conversation with a woman pushing a pram. My mother laughed, she knew all along about my father's fascination and adoration of babies. Later she repeated the story of the suspected affair and the comic discovery as a way of exploring this part of him herself. He is such an emotionally reticent man that this anecdote contained an element of her frustration. Her laughter at his idiosyncrasy contained more than a hint of irritation and loneliness.

I shake off these thoughts of my parents as they make me feel sad and hopeless and pinned to the floor. I shuffle around remoulding the material to reorient myself.

I am back in a comfortable nest, picturing myself as a sand-martin, no longer a cat but a bird in a bed made of its own feathers. The warmth of this fine duvet, a copy of the one made by the sand-martins over millennia surrounds me and I feel protected by history and the fact that creatures have forever been reproducing themselves. It is not sad or bad to have a child, or be a child. When Doug and I travelled to Vienna I experienced my first duvet, a white snowdrift on a vast double bed. I have enough room in my present nest for Doug and the baby and we are even cosier than our love nest in Vienna. In a nest buried in a sandbank the world is full of wonder. Talk about burying my head, but there's no turning back.

14. The Flydeck

DOUG THE FLYMAN

A few people are milling round, caught up in the immediacy of the tasks below. People have not returned from lunch so I have a little time to compose myself. They'll be back soon enough. The working lights are on the stage and in the auditorium. They must have been on all the time I was ruminating upstairs, my head in dense clouds. Were they on as I came down the stairs when I moved under the cover of darkness? I seem to be living inside my mind, constructing pictures of histrionic proportions while I no longer paint them. I have all but abandoned painting because life is so complicated, and making images takes up an inordinate amount of time. Too many relationships. Too much to contend with.

The self-portraits I attempted are morbid and self-indulgent, repulsively adolescent. The drawings of knives are much more interesting. Knives are extraordinary objects. Even the most ordinary knife has power and beauty. I should be able to take this fascination somewhere but it frightens me. The source of the fascination is too powerful, too compulsive. I feel I could turn the knives on myself. This frightens me. But I continue to draw them. I have a terrifying fear of dying lurking in my head. I have a daughter Becky who I adore. When I am with her I seem to forget everything. I have a terrifying recurring fear of her dying. The thought of her dying at any time before my life ends fills me with terror. I would rather take my own life. But this, too, terrifies me.

How has my love life become so complicated? I'm still married to Christine, who is one of my childhood sweethearts. Yet I always loved and still love Linda, who I have not seen for many years. I always will love her: the girl with red-brown thickly painted hair, its texture that of carefully handled impasto. She carefully bit her nails and methodically ate her favourite food and included the cores. I never tired of watching her every moment. I always wanted to fuck her. She went away to college and somehow I felt she had given up on me.

But even when Becky was born, I was seeing Mandy as often as I could. Now there is Jesse. The women are so different. Christine is dark, rather docile and boring, but her passivity I find arousing. The familiarity is dull but it can be strangely easy to have sex, to fit into old habits. Mandy was as fair as Christine is dark. She is vicious and cruel to me, a measure of her need and attachment, which is so often thwarted. I felt sad when I saw that her anger was waning, as it was a sign of her giving up on me. She had waited years and then she, too, gave me up and turned her anger into passion for James.

So now there is Jesse. I start to think about Jesse's body. She is petite and perfectly proportioned. There have never been such perfect breasts. Her skin is white, completely unblemished. The only fault I can find is a tiny red mark on the end of her nose. She is healthy looking; she radiates vitality and has a very slight layer of muscle on her compact frame. She is small-boned but still solid, like a beautiful smooth stone. Her skin glows. I love to watch her wander about naked in our small bedsit. I feel soothed thinking about her shape and smell. Each time I see her naked is a revelation. In intercourse it can feel as if we are one. But there is no sustaining this, we soon return to being separate, not synchronised. The feeling can only be sustained by more intercourse. It's like an obsession.

She surprised me when she drew me. She immediately got me, working feverishly with paper and pencil. She had instantly produced the sureness and squareness of my body. I did not know about this until she drew it. She barely looked at me as she did the drawing and completed it all in one piece in what seemed like minutes. It looked as if she had been studying me for a long time. It had an essential grasp of my form. I might never have a better portrait, essential elements of my shape and character captured in it. I know how important it is for artists to know the person drawn, to spend the required amount of time getting to know them. The intimate knowledge of the other's body, which does not have to come through sex; it could come through an intense period of looking and concentration. Only that could produce a good portrait. All artists who draw know this. Jesse had studied me enough in this intimate way and she could make the impression of me. I felt ashamed that I had only taken photographs of her. It seemed lazy, a cop out, as if I was afraid of an intimacy of this kind, a real connection.

Mandy was furious when she found out about Jesse. But she had refused to see me for some months. She said it was over. Mandy told me she had confronted Jesse and asked Jesse if she was seeing me. When Jesse said she was, Mandy told her that she had considered I was her property and was surprised at my new involvement. Jesse did not seem to care. She is so completely in love with me. I wish I were in her bedsit in Portobello Road eating her favourite supper of brie and salad made with avocados. I feel an intense need to possess her, wrapped up in her fierce body warmth. In one rapturous moment after an intense bout of fucking, Jesse had said that we – herself, Christine and Becky, the new baby and I, could all be together. I knew she meant it in that moment, but she would not be able to sustain it. Mandy had said something similar about the baby, but it became too painful and I could see the pain slowly turning into rage. Her face would break into myriad fragments of suffering and anger.

For a while it was Jesse who was bathed in the glow of warm tones and soft edges, with the mood of early love upon her, feeling no threat from anyone else in my life. It could not last and it didn't. Jesse has announced that she is pregnant. When I heard the news my mind simply reeled with the impossibility of the event. It was irreversible. I could see she was determined to go ahead with it. I had seen the same determination in Christine a few years before. I felt all my energy and creativity drain away. I am no longer important. I had felt the same when I had heard the news of Becky's conception. I felt shattered. And I can no longer hide behind the secrecy of the affair. A baby is something that cannot be hidden.

The news of Becky's birth hurt no one, least of all me. But it did something to me. I felt myself give myself over to the child. I emptied out. I love Becky. I would give everything to her, as I will to the new baby. Becky moves me beyond all else, and Jesse's baby will probably do the same. But I feel I can only exist for them. I can no longer exist for myself. When I am with Christine and Becky I feel myself as a burden, a spare part. I can be useful, and love the feeling of practicality, looking after the baby. I can find myself observing her and loving her but I feel my presence as dangerous. I feel I am too big and potentially harmful, too male, too much testosterone. How can I go through this again? The threat of the anger of the women pales into insignificance when the presence of a child takes me over in such a way as to make me lose myself. I feel deeply ashamed of this. I do not want to feel the children invading me but I cannot help it.

I can hear people coming back into the theatre. There is movement below on the stage and I stand up and look down and I see George moving around the desk. He is centre stage down at the front near the auditorium. He has been in and out as the set-up goes on and on. At the moment he is walking through the play by himself. Soon shouts come from the front of house telling people to take their positions. But they are still tinkering with everything. Eventually I will see the first red standby cue for the first act and I will draw the massive curtains that fill the proscenium. For the present I will continue to watch as the technical rehearsal moves slowly forward – and later on the dress rehearsal, and the evening performance. I am terrified for him. He is in danger of being possessed by Krapp. All the time, Krapp's voice will fill the stage, and I will attempt to block him out of my head.

I see Jesse come into the flies on the other side of the bridge. She is carrying a plastic bag. Something for me to eat, I guess. She has a box under her arm, something to drink. I now remember I asked her to get some beers and a sandwich. She has of course done my bidding. The bridge is narrow and it is easier to crawl on it than to walk, as the handrails are ridiculously low, suggesting the men who worked up here when the theatre was build were considerably smaller. Jesse is small but she would still find it difficult to walk across in an upright position. She has done this many times and moves in an assured way, carefully across the large gap. It is a long way at such a height. I wish she would fall. It would end all the agonies to come. I feel this rather than think it. It just comes out as a wish for everything to end.

Yet I am afraid. I cannot bear the thought of anything happening to her. She stops on the bridge. She is halfway across. The plastic bag seems to be hanging from her. Is she in danger of dropping it? It must be over her arm, surely. I feel a lurch in my stomach. She looks frozen on the spot. The box under her arm is at an angle and she is straining to look behind her. Her body looks rigid and twisted. I realise what is happening. The beers in the box are in danger of slipping out of the container. I have thought of this hazard before when I have carried stuff across myself. I freeze and feel suspended there with her. She is directly above the actor, George, sitting below her. He is caught up in his role, unaware of the drama unfolding above him. I realise it is my fault. I have willed it in some way. My body feels paralysed, mirroring her paralysis. I look at her in horror. I know that a can is a deadly missile if dropped from this great height onto the stage. This innocent missile could split the actor's head apart. I'm rooted to the spot. If I move or shout out I might disturb Jesse's concentration. I cannot anyway, my vocal cords are cemented like concrete. She is stone still. She is a woman on a tightrope high up on the building. At any point there could be a fall.

She is moving slowly. I think I can see her outline coming towards me in agonising slow motion. But I'm not sure. The noise below recedes. I can no longer hear it. She is starting to move forward, her progress only minutely apparent. It seems an age before she reaches the platform. She looks pale and frightened as her face comes towards me in the half-light from the stage below. She looks dazed. She briefly looks down at the stage and then turns sharply away from the edge and turns to go out of the door on to the roof. I fear she will fall off and I follow her outside as quickly as I can. I'm used to moving around without making any noise and I instinctively move in this way, even in the crisis.

Outside she is shaking. I ask her what has happened. She confirms, through sobs, that the beers had slipped out of the carton and wedged themselves behind her. Along the edge of the bridge runs an electricity cable and the cans were caught in the gap between them. Her sobs turn into animal sounds of pain, relief, fear and finally laughter. At last she is shocked and still. I hold her and the new baby. We sit on the roof's edge and eat the sandwich together. I keep in mind the rhythm of the day, knowing that there is still some time before I have to go back and attend to a possible waiting cue.

15. The Flydeck

DOUG THE FLYMAN

Jesse has gone and I am again sitting in the dark hearing voices, odd mutterings, nothing distinct, just me talking to myself. I went down to the wardrobe with Jesse for a few minutes and then escaped again. I climb high up into the roof of the theatre once more to a makeshift day bed where I can sink deep inside myself, away from Jesse and the other stagehands and the demands of the show, which alternate between tedium and compulsive effort. I close my eyes and the material world disappears.

I'm in a bedroom, my bedroom in the terraced house. The bed is small, a child's bed, but I'm in my adult body so it's a tight fit. The sheets are newly changed and tucked in around me, turned in and held in at each corner. I'm pretty terrified. There is a glow from the streetlights outside but this yellow cast only accentuates the darkness. I hear screaming coming from different directions. Sometimes it comes this way from the lane behind the backyard wall, sometimes that way, from over the terrace further away. The cries are all so similar, Mummy. Why does no one come and soothe them?

My mother is in the next room. I imagine I can hear her breathing, but she seems so far away, too far away to get a message to her. At least I'm in bed, tucked in so tightly I'm tied in, glad to have the sheets and blankets between me and the darkness. Would I be brave enough to look outside with the help of the sinister yellow light? If I could see something, perhaps I would be buoyed up enough to call her, and she would believe me, and not be angry because I've woken her. Would she want to know about the lost children outside? Dare I wake her bitter intolerance? Will she seem to love them and then change her mind, as she does with me?

There is play and laughter and then it falters and we fall backwards into shadow. The temperature changes and she is cold and empty. At times I see a blue energy coming off her and I know something bad is happening to us. I concentrate on the colour, tempering my fear. And it gradually fades. If I am brave enough to look out of the window I may be able to see the children and make her want to see them, too. If she can face them, maybe she can learn to face me, too, learn to look at my distress and still love me. I tell myself firmly that I can make this possible. I climb out of the sheets. It's not easy to loosen them. I'm in the cold, grey monochrome world of the night bedroom. Standing upright on the bed I can rest on the windowsill and push the limp, transparent curtains aside. I reach for the latch, an animal shape outlined against the yellowed dimness and open the window. The animal could be malevolent, it could bite me but I risk it and I feel buoyed up by my courage. It's icy and the wind pushes at me in a spiteful way, pulling air out of me in a gasp. My terror decreased as I moved, but it's back with the cold blast. Then I see it, the fire. It is leaping out of the window opposite, to the right. The screaming is coming from there, Mummy. I rush next door shouting, 'Mum-me please, Mum-me please.' I feel her body tower over me and lift me up back onto the bed. How can she lift my adult body so easily? She doesn't notice the changes in me. The remarkable change in my age and size. No surprises there. I also feel the firmness of her large hands as I'm tucked back into the sheets. It is all done swiftly and nothing is said. Nothing is to be done. The cries have subsided. Then curtly, 'There is no fire blowing, only the wind blowing a light bulb this way and that. Now go to sleep.' I'm not sure I believe it. It is plausible, I have to admit. But the memory of the cries and what I saw and felt remains the stronger vision. She always pushes me aside. She always says she puts me first but how can that be true? I never feel at the centre, always on the outside. Why should I believe her?

I've always been in terror of fire. More than once I've been a saviour sounding the fire alarm. I smelled fire in the big house when I was in bed, long before anyone else sensed it. We were on holiday in Blackpool and stayed in a boarding house. Sure enough, when they went further up the stairs they smelt it, too. An old lady had fallen asleep and knocked a candle over and the bed was beginning to smoulder. I was just in time for her, so they said. Another time I smelled it in the street and they were again sceptical. Once we were ahead, further down the street, we could see the smoke high up in a window. My mother likes to tell these stories, but not without an undertone of fearfulness and regret. She would be less happy if she knew about my dreams. I dream of wide open spaces and ordinary days, playing football in a field or walking down the lane; a huge cloud appears on the horizon and starts to come towards me. As it gets closer you can see it's a vivid red, and then I realise it's a ball of fire. I usually wake up crying for my father. Not Mum-me. Dad, dad, dad-de. He died, blown up in the war when I was ten months old. How did he die? Was it in a burning tank? A sinking ship? A stray bullet? The story is never consistent. I feel desolate. 'Ah, stop whinging,' one of the voices says, 'you're such a cry baby. You are so.'

There are only one or two photographs of my father and in both he looks small and insignificant and faded. Faded colour, as if he were a ghost already when the pictures were taken. He looks like no one else; so alien. It's hard to imagine any liveliness in pictures that are so small and vague. They are pictures he may not have kept if he were alive as they have so little to say about him. Sometimes I sense that he is with me in the dreams but only as a shadow. Even this slight presence fast disappears along with the future and I cry out in the empty night for Dad-de, Dad-de.

Without Dad there is just her and me. It would be OK except for this big hole in her. No one sees it as I do – just like the smoke and the fire. 'She adores you,' they all say that all the time. But it only stretches so far, this love. She cannot take any uncertainty or lack, or even quiet in me. She gets afraid – frantic. It's hard to describe it and I shouldn't bother to try. What's the point? The shifts are so subtle as to be barely there. If I had to swear an oath about it I might swear, but then again I might not be able to. She does not know about her absences, as far as I can make out. Once she is back from these gaps we carry on. It perplexes and troubles me, puts me at odds with myself. But once she is jolly and busy I can forget about it, just as she forgets what she never realised, was never consciously aware of in the first place. I, too, can completely forget about it for long stretches. The fun with her, the laughter, it can feel pretty real. At other times I am completely preoccupied with these emotional lacunae. I can see it in others and find it over and over again. Luckily it seems to divide into two places – the discomforting, unhappy awareness of the emptiness, and not thinking about it. And I find moments of excitement, which connect me to the real world. I know that other people have more of this feeling but I have much less of it.

There is always the two of us. We are inseparably bound together around His absence. In the wake of my birth came my father's death. She had to deal with the shattering of her happiness (or the illusion of it? What does it matter? It shattered). She had to deal with the knowledge that death is inevitable and that you do not know when it will come. My mother did not know about this until my father died. She had known death as a fact but not as a feeling. She could not know about mortality until losing Dad had taken away some part of her. I have known about death as a feeling from my beginnings. I saw it from my position in the womb. I could not understand it as a fact of life until I was what, eight? nine? I remember looking at his grave, realising that he was gone and that this would happen to everyone, including myself. From that moment I was terrified of death. I still am terrified that I and others will die. I can also wish them dead and be horrified by my own violence. It would seem that Sam has faced these terrors and has come to some conclusions about death and mortality. He seems to laugh in the face of it with his dark farce. I could do the same if I wasn't so burdened by fear. I am full of shame and, yes, dirt and sin. I am so ashamed that I cannot control my life.

Remy the stagehand told me Sam sees original sin, not as procreation, nor knowledge of sex. It is the actual coming into being of the child which is sinful. The child is an abomination because he is in a state of ignorance about death, and that is an abominable state. I was too young – a child absurdly free of the knowledge of death – to take in the facts after my father died. But I did know about it. I felt the fear from the off, from the moment I crept out of the womb. Remy told me that Sam blames the children for their ignorance, not their parents. I can feel he has a point, albeit seemingly a twisted one, because I do feel I'm to blame. I have felt it from the beginning, from as early as I can remember. I try to understand what it all means, this existence. I have read and read voraciously, followed the paths of ideas and theories, swallowing words like painkillers, an addict needing his fix. At times, notions fit together and seem to make sense of emotions, relationships, motives and the dynamics of life, but none of them makes me feel better long enough or takes away the guilt and self-hatred. Each day I try and I fail. I engage with the world and I expect things to get better and this is never the case. In this way, each day is like a death. There is only disappointment and loss. Everyday I die and am reborn, and I don't get any further. So I make a move to try to make others feel happy, as I cannot feel better myself. I resent this. It is a relentless cycle.

And Mother has told me in many ways how I could make her happy again. She lets me know that I could make up the loss of Dad if I was the way she wanted. But I cannot be a different person however much I try. And then, at other times she says I'm perfect, quite often in fact, before she switches back into silent disapproval and criticism. Can't Sam see it is not the child's fault? I want to be able to face the terrors of existence but Mother stopped me. She wanted me to abolish the terror by replacing it with a wish that fear and horror do not exist. I have to admit I am drawn to her position. I want to feel good with people, none of this other distressing nonsense. Once I dip down, it's impossible to make sense of the horrible feeling, as it is as bleak as the bleakest, dimmest, filthiest. When the cloud comes over me I'm all closed off. Inside my mind is a pitch black, pure horror. I can't be her companion, not even her friend, only a son doomed to disappoint her. Once I began to be aware enough to be afraid of my feelings she saw this and hated my weakness. It was then I became her companion in hell, an atmosphere where there is no evidence for any other existence. And then, she laughs and jokes! And we are off in another direction. She's mad. I'm humiliated. I had to get away from her without her seeing what I was doing. But she was devastated at my leaving her and my guilt and shame are endless torment. Can anyone else have felt this level of guilt at disappointing others they love? Has Sam? It's likely, but he must have escaped somehow. He has a key that I fear I will never have.

16. The Theatre Wardrobe

JESSE THE WARDROBE MISTRESS

People are watching us, talking about us probably, but they don't seem to judge or interfere. I am grateful to them for that at times, and at other times wish I had someone to talk to whom I could trust. At worst I can feel I am in a play or novel, moving towards an unknown ending. I am watching myself wondering where this is going and how will it be. None of our younger group has any children except Stephen, the father of Rose. Doug already has a child so he knows where we are going. There is no need to see it as precarious. The lighting man's wife has talked to me as if she were trying to warn me of some likely disaster, which is a bit much. She seems a pretty miserable person with an axe to grind about her husband. No wonder he works here all the time. She made me think that Doug might leave me, which was terrifying. But he is not going to do that. He is too good a person. Still, I can feel our lives are in transit and I'm travelling without much of a plan and I'm scared. In this way it does resemble the plays, all is heightened life force, emotionally driven, but who knows where? We do know where we are going. To live in a provincial town and start a new life there while I study and look after the baby, and Doug works; our future home a large student flat, but he seems OK about that.

No point analysing actions and choices, which are as irreversible as a baby on its way. The plays, those in rehearsal downstairs, are made to be analysed. A man and a woman in two separate unconnected stories, both alone and full of charged, pained memories. Watching the rehearsals again and again I've been thinking about the man's reaction to the tape when it describes him with his lover in the punt. It is a point of recognition but this contact is so conflicted in that he both longs for it and recoils from it. It is so bleak and so full of yearning. He dismisses this longing, which is pretty chilling. His life seems over, pared down to a few remnants, but he is defiant, triumphant even. He has stripped everything from himself. He has done this injury to himself. He should be a pathetic figure, repulsive even, yet he is neither. He is an enigma. He is a figure in a picture, where words do not add a narrative or explanation; the words fill in more detail of the man's inner life and heroic loneliness. He lives on. The construction of the play is simple, stark, striking, compelling just like a visual representation. The visual is made out of words. Doug helped me understand this. He has shown me so much about his world of painting and art. I cannot understand how he can know so much and be so passionate about it, then at other times find it pointless. 'No point in going in that direction,' he says. 'It is closed to me.' I don't think he really means this. He is a bit low but will pick up once we're away from the city and all the complications with Mandy.

I have already had a chance to see some of the plays because I have nothing much to do once the shows start. Once they are running I will be down there watching every night. I can see myself there at every performance. Standing in the wings I'm so close to the action of the play that I imagine myself a part of this closed world and its intensity. No one watching in the theatre will be as close or feel it as I do. I am already soaked in the drama. They are beyond characters, beyond novels, beyond narrative, beyond words. It is not a play but a living, breathing action of rhythm, silences and sound. I breathe with the actors – a gripping meditation.

In *Not I*, a witness stands to one side of the stage, listening to a disturbed woman's twelve-minute tirade. The words are disjunctive, broken up, but their gist comes through loud and clear, strands of living tissue separated with a wire brush. My hair stands on end. I am enrapt, engrossed as well as alert for any cue that means I'm needed somewhere else. It is as if I am in my sleep, with one set of antennae ready for a baby's cry. Also I can look up into the darkness and know that Doug is up near the roof. I look into the darkness of the play and at the dark shape of my lover and yet I am so full of joy and hope.

I don't linger on the difficulties, just as I do not linger on the morbid qualities in the play's content. My joy is dominant. I am so close to new life that I cannot take the emptiness seriously. Both the passivity of the marijuana and the deathly repetitiveness in the plays are frightening. I won't tolerate it. So I allow myself to be more taken up with the energy and drive of the drama conveyed by the words and man's unpredictable movements.

My hope helps me to see beyond my situation. Doug is married and has a young daughter whom he adores. He has left his wife and he is with me and I wish I could somehow make the circumstances different. I cannot feel guilty about the end of his marriage. He says it has always been difficult, about sex and nothing else. She had been his childhood sweetheart and he had gone back to her when he lost Linda, his first real love. I understand him. I had also been totally besotted with someone who'd disappeared. It had been terrible and I thought I could never feel better. I do know that I am with him and am going to make sure he feels happy and whole again, as I do with the baby. He would see Becky as much as possible and in time the families will have to work something out. At the moment it is all in transition and he's frightened at times. I can see this. But nothing can shake my conviction. What could make me waver when I love him so completely and am carrying his baby?

I can see he is struggling. This is not really a clear thought but a feeling that I encounter in myself as part of him. I cannot see this as a threat to our future. It is only a state to be weathered and born. It is too contradictory. I can't keep two opposites in my mind. No, that is not true. I do have doubts and encompass them with a forceful energy that neutralises. I have to do so because of the threat to the baby's existence and myself.

A few days before, I had seen him in the alleyway. I see him there all the time as we pass by each other in the working day. I see him in all parts of the building and in the spaces around it. He was standing looking preoccupied and lost, and I approached him.

He said that he had been talking to his friend, a woman he was at art school with, and he said, without taking a breath, that he thought he could now leave me. He felt that perhaps he could be strong enough to do it. I was shaken. Every fibre of me wobbled and shook. No part of me was untouched. I burst into tears. He could not be serious that he was leaving the baby and me. I looked at him in disbelief. Where had this come from? Seeing me in such a state he caught hold of me and took me out to sit by the canal opposite. We sat on a bench under the lime trees. It was quite dark, even with the streetlights. People were busily crossing the bridge, on the way home; they took no notice of us. I felt I was in a corridor separated from the world. I was in a corridor of pain. Doug put his arms around me to comfort me, comforting himself. It was OK he said. He could just get overwhelmed. He did not say this. But I felt it.

This is what I want to believe. His big body sat next to mine and once again his presence felt like a rock made out of cool, finely carved stone. Unquestionably, he is moulded for me. Will I later wonder about his stability? So much speaks out against him, and others like Mandy and the electrician's wife want to join the chorus. He had been unfaithful to his wife a number of times already. Why should it be different for me? Well, it is different. If only they could see it. There is no one else for me. Doug is full of deep hurt, there is a huge need inside him, and it is a hole that has to be filled. His history is one of infidelity. I can only hope I will be enough for him now. Why does that not stand a chance? Part of me takes me to the side to say *look long and hard at your position*. But it is only a tiny part. The electrician's wife had tried to push me towards believing I was deluding myself about him. I had blotted out the painful reality of his instability. She called him a womaniser, which is absurd. He is not malicious or conniving. He is muddled.

The next day went on as usual. It was as if the conversation in the alleyway had not happened. I was relieved it was a Sunday. We had risen late and Doug had drawn and photographed me resting on the bed. We made love and went to a gallery in the afternoon.

It was a Picasso exhibition. I had started to understand something of the many faceted figures, particularly the crazy, distorted, weeping women. Picasso's perspective was close in, extremely close. He drew a millimetre away from his unfortunate subjects, the women he loved and hated. He could make his lovers extremely miserable and then draw them in close up, everything exposed. He had observed his precedents, the Spanish carvers who cut out the facets of the weeping Christ and his Virgin Mother. The rage and the distortion of loss, I can see it so clearly and my heart goes out to them.

I am less sure of the colour. What about the pink woman? Picasso's younger lover for whom he deserted his ballerina wife? She was all glowing pinks and yellows.

'Think about the fact that they have just fucked,' said Doug rather abruptly, as if I should have understood immediately. Sometimes I can feel Doug's angry, impatient side. Others talk about his ideals and his uncompromising personality. The other men backstage admire this. They are slightly fearful of him. He has this kind of questioning look. He would take up a particular body position when he disagreed with the others. His head would be cocked to one side, his eyes piercing, not so much in judgment or criticism but oppositional, polemical, challenging. As if to say,

'Think of what you are saying and the careless way you are positioning yourself.'

We had listened to music. We both like John Lennon. We talked about the falling out between Paul and John. I said that to hate him so much meant he must love Paul. Doug hugged me. He said he loved it when I said things like that. He likes the things I think about and he says he likes the way I talk to people. He said he loved my mind as much as my body and I laughed because him saying that made me so happy. He had wondered what my body would be like under the layers of my kaftan. He had been excited and delighted with my thighs when I wore my pink mini dress and long boots. He said he was so surprised and knocked out by how perfectly proportioned I am. He adores my breasts. He says they are perfect. I feel so utterly loved, and in love. I feel, too, that he has the most perfect mind and body. He always interests me and everything he says seems right. Physically he is so handsome and his body so square and strong. His moustache is funny and his hair so dark and wavy. When I am with him, we are not mortal. We are gods.

A friend said to me, 'He is so old! When he is older he will be like one of those old men in a working men's cap and jacket.' I was shocked. How insensitive and contemptuous! Doug did wear working men's clothes, like all the other stagehands; jeans and a dark working man's cloth jacket in the winter. I could see she might be right. But this is talking light years away. I'd be older, too. *When I get older, losing my hair, many years from now...* I will adore him when he is old. His beauty will be a memory I will carry for him. I will still see him as he is now, even in his faded features and thickened body. Unlike Mr Krapp, I will never let my love go.

A blank: I draw a blank, a blank feeling, a not feeling, as if I have come to the end of a winding path, the ones that look like endless branches of tree roots in drawings of the brain. Doug once made these drawings. He sat and drew them for me rather than describe them. Our situation has to work out somehow. There is too much passion for it not to be possible. How does a baby get in the way? How could it? People have said it is going to be extremely hard, feeding the baby around the clock. I know they're exaggerating. I am young, for God's sake, barely beyond twenty. It is not possible to work but there is a place at university. It has come at the perfect time. They won't know about the pregnancy at first. Once things are settled, I will tell them of course. A bunch of academic, intellectual liberals are not likely to throw a woman and a baby out. They will help. The facilities for students studying with children are good. I have a grant, quite a lot of money actually. I, too, can carry on growing while the baby is small. Doug has a job in the town, in the theatre there. Lodging with a friend in a small town nearby looks like a promising start. There is just so much to look forward to, literature, more plays, and philosophy. We are so lucky that so much is coming together. I am not orchestrating it. It has a life all of its own.

Others try to tell me that I am in over my head. Liz the electrician's wife said I needed to be careful of a man like Doug. How dare she? It is obvious that she feels pushed out of the crowd at work. She is a wife on the periphery of close and amorous work, friendships and loves. She is jealous and angry, but why direct it at me and Doug? We had started to be friendly and then I had less time because of Doug. A bit of guilt rises up, but why? She has her husband and family. Though I don't envy her Jerry. Still, I feel a bit tearful. I didn't want to hurt her by being unavailable. Hell, I can't be responsible for everyone. I can no longer be friends with her because of her vileness towards Doug. Am I getting too emotional? Must be the hormones. I have not done anything. I can't do any more. There is enough on my plate. No more thinking about this!

It is hard to put together Sam and his plays. He is so unlike his characters. The people in the plays are extremely cut off and lonely – devoid of any warmth or contact. But Sam is a warm character and it's easy to feel you are accepted by him. He does not seem to discriminate. I can see he could be hard on you if you let him down. George has rubbed him up the wrong way, that's for sure.

It's easy to see the emptiness in the plays as part of the pared down self. Dreams feel like this. You are there in them but as a presence. Dreamscapes can be landscapes, shantytowns or urban settings, mass tenements, or houses in states of rebuilding or decay. My own dreams are full of this kind of landscape. A longing to engage is constantly thwarted. I suppose this is why I feel like an additional character in the plays when I can watch so closely. The play becomes an extension of my own inner world. Whatever happens, the feeling left is a satisfying sadness. But then I want to oppose the play and say there is truth there about emotional and existential existence but it is not the whole truth, not the whole story. His people are stripped down to their aloneness, fragility, anger, and small bites of humour, thank goodness.

Sam is most unlike his plays and most unlike anyone else I've ever come across. His demeanour, his poise, his quiet authority are much more than age or maturity. It is hard to believe he's in his sixties. Remy says he has grandeur and this has to be related to the facing of his own inner darkness. Remy is convinced that this has come through the descent into himself. Out of that encounter comes, paradoxically, an extraordinary calm and certainty. Both Doug and Remy have been reading Jung. The language is extremely hard going for me, so I am grateful for their summaries. We all love Sam. He feels like such a good man – firm, calm and reliable. He is able to sit still like a monk, a quiet active presence. He is extremely funny and wickedly forthright in a way that makes it hard to take offence. It's easy to feel settled when he is in my room going through the button boxes.

Sam would never give you the kind of look Doug gives others. He seems to take everything into himself. His head looks as if it has had to enlarge to deal with the capacity of his brain. He looks like many other writers and actors. Huge heads, like Picasso's, made out of crags and planes carved from the inside out. Larger than life brains belonging to a separate species, the intellectual, evolutionary species ahead of their time. Doug has this capacity. If only he wasn't so taken over by other things. I've not seen much of his artwork. It is all in his old home with that wife of his. It has to be good. What I have seen moves me. He would only be able to produce something good or important. He understands art, having studied it for years. He's older than me, twenty-nine, but he only left art school a few years ago. He studied for years so he must have got somewhere with it. All this work to support his family was getting in the way – and now another baby is coming.

Sam has greatness in him. His experiences differ from others and he has a need to express this. He said as much. He had struggled to get his work accepted and to make a living when he was young. My talks with Doug suggest many artists found it hard to lead ordinary lives and to produce their art. Sam has a wife and a mistress. His mistress, so Remy tells me, is English. His wife is French. I think he said she is French. They have no children. Had they decided not to have children? It would make things easier, perhaps.

Virginia has children. She has four. They are grown up now. And she had not worked when they were small. She started her career in design when she was in her forties. Doug said he is too caught up in his responsibilities to do any creative work. This will change. Once we are settled down he will be able to do what he is meant to do. He needs a clear space, he says. We will make a clear space. I know that Doug is like Sam, that he is going to do something special. He is going to do something extraordinary. People around him find him a bit edgy, a bit above them, but they love him. Two black clad legs have appeared in front of me. Damn – it's Janet.

'Jesse, what are you doing under my desk'?

' Sorry, just having a nap – forty winks – I felt a bit tired. But I feel better now. Thank you.'

' I think you should go downstairs and see what is happening, don't you?'

I get up, smoothing my imaginary blue dress and apron, squeeze past Janet and casually comb my hair, walking down the stairs.

AFTERNOON TECHNICAL

17. The Theatre Stalls

VIRGINIA THE DESIGNER

The Technical moves extremely slowly as George paces out the play for everyone else to practise putting the props and cues in place. The lighting will take a while. Once again I peruse the set. It seems to have the right qualities, an atmospheric black ground waiting for the live, tormented figure that will inhabit it. But the stage is empty at the moment and Peter is in the stalls and in the foulest of moods. I am consequently in touch with myself as the child called Virginia, as I sit in the auditorium looking at his back. He has been prowling around in the stalls, his temper a palpable cloud hanging around, a purple aura that others, including me, are keen to avoid. He is a tall man but seems to have filled out lately and takes on the proportions of a giant towering above the landscape; hence my feeling so small.

My father could be as volatile as Peter and I learnt to protect myself early on from his more violent emotional undercurrents. These would erupt unpredictably when he felt under pressure. My father, like Peter, was brilliant, likeable, charismatic and unable to tolerate certain types of foolish behaviour and ignorance, and unfortunately, certain types of vulnerability. He, like Peter, did not always have sympathy or the ability to appreciate the emotional complexity of others' problems. Lack of an immediate response to something he needed you to understand, appalled him, and rather than shrink from it, as you might wish him to, he would attack. The colour of vulnerability, its milky-white, bluish presence, acted as a signal and he would pounce, prompted initially by fear and revulsion, quickly taken over by its propellant, anger. He did not distinguish between different types of weakness. What he saw as weak needed to be got rid of as soon as possible. My father did not always have a continuum of variants in his mind regarding others' attempts to understand the world and its complexities. He did not distinguish between wilful or thoughtless stupidity, or of not being informed, or not able to formulate, so it became necessary to make these distinctions myself. No one else was there to do it for me so I had to decide what was useful in his harsh relentless anger and criticism, and what I needed to disregard. I had to ask myself, 'Is there anything reasonable in all this hurtful stuff?' I remember, even as a child, feeling the blast and examining its effect on my emotions, and my body. It hurt me physically. Something sinister flooded through me. The red, bluish bruising colour of the visceral flooding muddied my whole range of thinking and feeling. The colour range of my sensibilities would feel obliterated and I would struggle to rebuild my original palette of love, hate, fear, sadness, anger. Sometimes I would give up, and search for resonant sounds instead. If I could sense a clear sound in myself, I could start to get a sense of what I was feeling and build some equilibrium around it.

If my thoughts, voiced or felt, were experienced in opposition to some essential part of my father, I could feel a wave come over him, and then over me, as powerful as a tsunami. I would feel myself drowning, flooded with heat, but I learnt that I could gradually struggle to the surface. This knowledge would be strangely certain and uncertain at the same time. It was certain that his airiness and clarity would return to him, and to us. It might be minutes, hours or days. But the time it took him to reach this had a dreadful, timeless quality. This timelessness felt so real and could be endless – so that the knowledge of the inevitable release from the anger and counter anger was not convincing. It was both certain and uncertain, the uncertainty taking the upper hand. It was a paradox brought about by parallel experiences.

Peter's temper is the result of having one of the two plays taken out of his hands, as well as a frustrated relationship with George. While we had time, and therefore hope, he kept going without resorting to this temper. Having had a lifetime of gauging when a man might blow, I guess that this is about to happen. George is protecting himself, working by himself with himself. For some reason he cannot find anything with Peter. When Sam gave him notes in the beginning, George would look to Peter for confirmation. This was the correct protocol, but Sam unfortunately was deeply offended by it. But Sam does not seem to have been convinced by the casting from the start. The choice came from the need to have a star and this probably rankles. I don't think David would have allowed this to happen. It is unfair to ask a performer to play because he is famous and can make money for the theatre, and then dislike him for this. I tried to approach George, just to see if talking could loosen up the situation, but he brushed me off. I was upset and alarmed to see that George is so hurt or despairing of the situation that he just wants to keep himself in his own space. It is a need for love when extremely vulnerable that cannot be talked about because it cuts so deep. It is the need for the actor to have the director fall in love with him. Not romantically, not sexually. But as a parent loves a child and can let them be and encourage them to find themselves in the task. No matter how big a performer is, he or she needs this. In this case, without this alchemy, the actor cannot be certain of himself, or, in this case, has to rely only on himself. Without this love, which David had an endless capacity to give, it is not certain what kind of performance will emerge. It is unfortunate that George has been forced into himself in this way. I can see that he has been giving the rehearsals all he can but he is isolated in his endeavour.

When I tried to tell my father something of my feelings about the world, how I saw what was important, I was often taken aback by how much it offended and hurt him. Of course, this had not been my intention. I wanted to engage him in conversation that meant something to us both. I wanted to show myself to him. Discovering that my differences from him could hurt him was devastating. This was when I became more conscious of the fact that I thought in colours. The palate and intensity could subtly or dramatically change. My emotions would arise with a defining feel of a colour. I could feel my anger rise to meet his; a hot element of red (blood red, of course) adding to the colour mix, the colour run, the colour mass. It was sickening. I could not escape him so I needed to find a way to manage the impact he had on me. I learnt to separate out other colours, which took on shades differing from the red flush.

This meant holding onto the fracturing feelings of having hurt him, while gradually letting myself see that this was not my fault. When I was younger this would make me feel beside myself: in agonising pain. But I gradually realised that it was inevitable. There was nothing I could do to prevent it. I could not help him. It was the painful part of my relationship with him. I was simply wrong, the wrong kind of daughter; at times when I could not mirror him, agree with him, adore him, it would devastate and inflame him. George, at this crucial moment, has no love for Peter and vice versa. And they are both furious with each other, with nothing between them to break the cycle of blame.

My father was a writer, I'm a painter, a visual thinker, and a person who thinks and feels more through images than words. I could not be like him, I was his daughter, not even a son with whom he would at least have had maleness in common. Would that have helped? A son could do no better unless he gave himself over to being entirely like his father. No child, without seriously injuring itself, could fulfil this relentless destiny. The only choice I had was to survive it. So I would calm myself and examine what he was saying about me in his relentless criticism and work out what I could use from it. I was always surprised at how it would hone something new, focused, shiny and bright in my own understanding of myself. How did this miracle happen?

I could totally disagree with him, hate him, wish he would have a heart attack and disappear. All the time the exchange was happening I could feel the need to get rid of the intensity – to get rid of him. And yet, his hurt, his need, his completely impossible position, my love and sympathy for him, my appreciation of his complexity (he could be so loving, generous and understanding), his vulnerability, his wounded feelings, all this kept him with me and enabled me to take on something from his position which strengthened mine. This merging with him brought about richer colours and sounds in my mind. I often wondered how I had been able to do this when I was younger. It was no more complicated than a capacity for self-preservation. Somewhere I had been given permission to be myself and I eventually realised that it had been from the same source that had opposed me so strongly, my father. He feared my difference because it suggested that he would lose me entirely. But despite this, he also saw that he had to let me be myself. He would swing between these two possibilities, sometimes in a seesaw of wild mood swings. Times were volatile and unpredictable when the stakes were high between us.

I recognise this in all the powerful men I have worked with in this theatre. They, too, could be vicious when the stakes were high. I can see this as a possibility in all three men – Sam, George, Peter. Even the most even-tempered, most charming and personable directors would be ruthless when they felt that something precious for them in the work was being challenged. I could see these points of rupture as potentially the most creative ones if both parties could meet. I have become adept at manoeuvring at these crucial points, but my knack is absent right now.

Earlier I watched Peter tear a strip off one of the stage managers who had made a mistake about the sequence in a rehearsal. Jane looked terrified, but had seen an opportunity to put in a lighting run planned for later in the day. I imagined that this might suit her temperament better, giving time to sort out the technical nuts and bolts. She seemed surprised when Peter let it go. So here was an example of how staying with your own focus helped to weather a clash with someone much more powerful.

George seemed completely out of tune earlier in the day. Was he tired? Peter called for a break and when he came back asked George to change his rhythm, 'to slightly up the tempo,' he said. This worked wonderfully for a moment, as it helped a subtle narcissistic mania to emerge, which gave his Krapp a more comic edge. Peter did not attack him even though the right nuance for the performance is eluding George and the opening performance is looming. It has been known for miracles to happen.

I never felt that my father would make a gear change for me. Is that fair? He would take the pressure off but never hand me something as directly as Peter handed George this kindly direction. What I do feel with Peter is that if I made a mistake or did something at odds with him, he would respect my struggle to meet him and he would hand me a direction, too. He would facilitate me, not crush me. My father never entirely crushed me. I suppose that's it. He wanted to mould me and he wanted to own me, but he did not want to destroy me. This is what I see in all the powerful men around me. They are ruthless in their determination to shape the productions, but they need others around them who equally have a purpose or vision to fulfil, and who need them just as much. This forging of work through others I learnt from my father.

I watched my own son, Martin, earlier in the week and thought about how he helped me to repaint the sets when he was a child. He came to my rescue many times when I had to completely repaint sets because technicians in the past refused to take my designs seriously. It took a while to educate the set builders who had done things in a different way for so long. All four of my children were delighted at first, then more grudging, as they grew older. They are too old now to do my chores – but I always feel good when they are around. My body seems to relax and I feel free to get on with the tasks around me. It would infuriate them to know that I can completely forget about them when they are within my orbit, almost within sight. I can feel even more absorbed with the demands of the production. They had so many holidays as dogsbodies in the theatre, fetching and carrying, even doing some paid work.

When Martin got older, he started to challenge me. He jibed about 'my men' at the theatre. He said I had them all under my thumb. This is a young person's simplification, but my hackles rose. I've worked for this position. I've fought, not just for my designs, but the day-to-day emotional battle to get others to see my ideas, and to see how I can integrate other people's concepts when I'm not entirely sure what those other concepts mean. I thought this but didn't say it, of course. I suppose Martin has felt that he has had to battle for my attention. He is clever and he and his sister are close, so I left them to get on with it. What kind of father did I find for them? What kind of father and mother have I been to them? That is for them to decide. I don't know if it's possible to do that kind of thinking for other people, particularly your children.

Martin taunted me about being the theatre's mother. There's something in that. I create the space, a container for all that goes on in the plays. It reminds me of another of Martin's digs, 'Mother Courage.' But all the same, David and I agreed with Sam. We knew that each element in the play had to come from the written word, from the plays themselves, each tiny detail had to be given equal weight, each element resonating. What would David or Sam think of the idea of the container?

The space on the stage is where it all happens and I dress everyone. I feel a great pleasure in what I've created. It is mine – and I deign to share it. I look at the stage and imagine my children playing on it, a vast playhouse. I feel David's presence. I feel the reality of my position in the theatre and the responsibility I feel for the space, my home. I have been working here for seventeen years. David and I forged this place in a consensus. It fitted together, and now it hangs there; for not only does it come from painstaking work but from miraculous energies.

Will it hold together? This seems to be the question on Peter's mind. There is one new play and an established one in the balance. The final work of the rehearsals and the way it acts as a catalyst is not yet done. Moving the components into the final space is always cumbersome. The endless technical rehearsal suggests it can never have a flow, never have the intimate concentration it had in the rehearsal room. How do people tolerate work on films? They plan and trust the pieces will fit into place over many months. It's a Herculean task. I am feeling protective today! Perhaps it's the presence of the children who are now separated from me. They are free of me now and I am free of my anchor. Does that make me happy? I used to think that it would but am not so sure just now. I'm not sure why I feel some impending doom, and the need for someone particularly close to me like David or my father or the children. What makes this so important? My feelings and preoccupation with family seem puzzling. Productions are always difficult.

But David, my dead dear, you are sorely needed at the moment. I need to tell you that I feel afraid of what I know not. I'm unnaturally rattled by what I have experienced many times before – productions that are yet to come alive. I find it impossible to put my finger on why there is such a funereal atmosphere. What is happening to the energy which I always expect to find during the last day?

I remember coming back to the theatre after looking after the family for a long time. Making props, masks and sets gave me a particular liveliness again. I could give myself over to the work and it would take me to a place inside myself, free of outside demands – those tiresome domestic needs. David, you did for me what you did for anyone, you encouraged me to inhabit myself. You trusted that by doing, and by absorbing yourself in the demands of the others involved, it would be possible to create all you could and something bigger than yourself. These syntheses are not smooth or painless. They have all kinds of rough textures. They are full of struggle and uncertainty. But I never had to fight with you. We set ourselves apart from other people and worked as an entity.

Thinking of you is still painful. I move into a vast absence. It is more a physical feeling than an emotional one, as if I've had you removed from me, and yet you are like a phantom limb. At present your absence has an extremely raw quality. How my breath inevitably quickens and exacerbates the ache. Strange to feel so much swelling absence, when you are all around me in the theatre where we worked for ten years together. I constantly want you to see where our project is taking me. I want you to see all that has been made of our theatrical home. No, I only want you to see what I have made of it! My breathing becomes rapid and I can feel my heart as a heavy substance. My diaphragm works to lift it. It is heavy with sorrow and work – a good feeling, satisfying because it is made of real anguish. I do feel I am carrying you, David, in my trunk, quite literally. It is a burden that I would never abandon. My children did – and do – complain that they do not come first, but how can anyone come first in another's deepest inner life?

I feel both energised and tired, and wish I could go home for a while. I feel I need a break. I have been in the theatre for days now. Maybe I will go home. I can see myself sitting in the kitchen. It is reasonably tidy but not very clean. This does not bother me. I have all the bits and pieces that I need around me, the collected erotica, flora and fauna of my kitchen. The pleasure of functional design is everywhere I look. It is always busy at home with people sitting, eating and drinking. Delicious food is easy to throw together. I can always escape to my studio to work if I need to. No one now questions my need to make things.

I marvel at how my father's and mother's lives unconsciously dominated once upon a time; I had to be married, to have children, to be an adult. I needed to recreate the stability I had known as a child with my own family and children. The children might scoff at first if they heard that, but then I think they might see that it's true. I had eschewed this path for a time as a young woman, but part of me was extremely lonely. When I met my husband and had my children I could inhabit, as fully as possible, my parents' world. I had all they had, a stable home and an environment designed for a family, which was alive with the everyday richness, chaos and the grind of a household. I'm a working person; the value of work could not be greater. Both my mother and father were busy social people, their lives full of career and obligations. I took this on undigested. I ate it whole.

My first family had the life of a creative family living in a particular time and class: professional, married, educated, cultured; following family tradition, bohemian, unconventional, Bloomsbury-like. I had always fantasised about living at Charleston when I first discovered the Omega Workshops. I mentioned this once to an old school friend. 'How could you want to live there?' she said, 'they are chaotic dirty people.' Yes, they are, I thought, and my house is none too clean. How could it be with so much to do? Art and children; one glorious, messy, chaotic business. It became messier once I took up with David.

A friend, the French woman and I, were talking about being abroad. She said that she was surprised at the English middle classes abroad. 'They live like peasants,' she said, in a pleasant questioning rhetorical voice, 'don't they?' She may have been a little worried about offending me. Or maybe she did not seem to quite include me in this. I loved to live in the rustic charm and disorder of a holiday house in the south of France, following in the footsteps of Vanessa, and Virginia, my namesake.

I would love to have had a house with colour and serious decoration evident on every surface. I had to be content with there being others' beautiful design and craft. My serious decorating goes on in the theatre. Still, I could have a fantasy of painting my environment and family, escaping to the studio to work with the model. This kind of fantasy I recognise as one where the mind needs to exercise, expanding for the sake of it: a sort of stretching.

I look up at the black set, with its freshly painted surface shining under the working lights. The crew and George are moving about slowly. This pleases me because I can remember when I first used this particular kind of set and I still enjoy the way the real space comes through. The set is modernist, minimal and abstract and yet it is still working hand in hand with painters who forged the way, like Watteau, Goya and Gainsborough; all competing sensibilities who made the way for clarity and fluidity. The blackness is the ground for the figure and will resonate with the man in the play whose life has been stripped down to an unbearable, comic minimum; a grotesque sympathetic display. This modernist space sits in the frame of a Victorian proscenium arch, a heavy gilt frame of another century, much like the nineteenth century modernist painters were displayed in the trapping of baroque eighteenth century gilt. This historical framing adds serious weight and context to the present solemnity. Gilt plaster flowers surround the proscenium, and its fruits and figures are covered in the paint of many years' redecoration. These blend with the accompanying Victorian seating and wallpaper. All this becomes the historical frame around the set, which is my modern painting. All is set for the human drama to come. I am dreading something and I have waves of sickness almost. What is it? Shame? I need to shake this off.

18. The Theatre Stalls

PETER THE DIRECTOR

What makes me hesitate? It is the fact that George's work has been without obvious fault. He has been word perfect from the off. Not at all easy with this sort of script and he tries to stick religiously to the text and its instructions. He is giving a performance with emotional range. It just isn't an exceptional performance yet, which is what is expected of him. Sam wants him to listen more to his instructions, also to instruct him beyond the hard facts on the page. But he refused that from Sam, and from me when I tried to take a more Sam-like stance. I understand about the different pacings needed for the narrative's speech, different tempos, some lyrical, others harsh and sardonic. These give us the story of the radically different parts of the old man's character. But now I'm stuck and nothing I do helps him in this impasse.

So, with nothing else available, I substitute this crazy business that is churning around in my head. And George is presumably struggling to work out what is so displeasing for me. George can see my vexation, chagrin, resentment and he, like me, does not know what to do with it. It is a claustrophobic situation, just the two of us. He is equally fed up with me. I'm dreading the rehearsal. There is no distraction. I had hoped that moving the play out of the rehearsal room into the theatre where we have to think about all the technical problems would dilute this tension.

I am also convinced, and I am not sure why, that there has to be more than demonic anger in this character. His body needs to be imbued with a whole range of expressed and unexpressed disappointments and his iron determination to survive. He is full of a kind of contempt which could destroy another man. I am stuck with an overwhelming conviction that the core of the character projects rage, guarding against feelings of disintegration and loss. I am unable to experience anything else at this time. I know he is more than that, but I can't articulate anything more complex in myself, or to George. It is not that George's performance is awful. He is more than a seasoned actor. Krapp is a burnt-out hull containing a contradictory mass of powerful self-hatred and scorn; mixed for good measure with wily intelligence and ordinary, poignant comic responses. Our man has lost all, but is full of raw unstable energy, constantly disintegrating and re-integrating before us. He is moving towards entropy but not without a fight. It has to become an unconscious attitude, its expression carried through the body. This is how I understand Sam's need to stick with the text, and the moves he dictates, to allow them to carry the shifting cadences, nuances, the pauses, the tone, the silences, the stresses of a life force. It has to be obvious like carnival or pantomime, more archetypal and mythical than pure id. This character has been stripped of his worldly assets including any beauty he may have had. George has a strong handsome face and presence, which just now suggests the opposite. I am right about the mask. It is a good metaphor. Sam strips down his characters to mask-like entities. He asks them to speak through the text as if were a mask. The actor has to find the struggling inner life without a face and without a response. This is taken to its logical conclusion in Krapp, a man who is separate from society – and alone. There is no one to relate to except himself and his own voice on the tapes.

I think of Matisse's wife in *Portrait of Mme Matisse*. He had her sit over a hundred times and later, seeing the painting would make Amelie Matisse weep. As a sitter she would be the recipient of her husband's ruthless scrutiny. And she changed her face into a mask which he faithfully recorded. All kinds of feelings are refined and transmitted through every part of the picture, not through the oval mask like face, but all the brush marks and plastic colour, the equivalent of Sam's words. It's the orchestrated colour in the painting that gives us Mrs Matisse. It is easy to read into it the tempestuous aspects of the Matisse marriage.

For the painter and sitter it would be an exhausting, even gruelling experience and I feel like this myself with the actors at the moment. George has shut down to protect himself. Anna is in agony, trussed up in darkness where she loses her bearing and is in fear of losing her mind. She and Sam argued against me about the slower pace I wanted and I saw that it was reasonable to capitulate for the play, but unsure if it was a reasonable decision for Anna's sanity. Anna's speaking turns the words into sound and this tears at your guts and turns you upside down, as does the experience of watching in almost complete darkness. You lose your visual and mental bearings. George seems to have shut down inside. Could this be a reflex, a protection against mental disintegration? Anna has been on the verge of a breakdown. Yet she carries on and does not give up. I see it is risky, but, surely this is what we are here to do? I wish I could place a mask, or a bag, over George's head and be done with it. I realise this is churlish, but these thoughts give vent to my frustration without doing any obvious harm. People have occasionally said my temper is extremely destructive but I don't see it myself.

I'm distracted by a young man, Doug, walking across the set and sitting at Krapp's desk. He is doing something with the drawers that face towards the audience and he starts to do some work to the drawer, just like Krapp. In this way he seems to be unconsciously mimicking the business of the play. Krapp keeps all his tapes and bananas in the drawers and has to reach over the four-legged creature to get to his props. This is one of the wonderful aspects created by Sam. It is one of many light touches that speak about the difficult struggle in Krapp's relationship with himself.

Doug sits at the desk. He is dressed in black so he could almost be in costume. He is doing nothing other than sitting, but sadness and anger leak out of him. His body is trapped like a caged animal. He looks defeated but ready to kill. He is a tall person, but his fitness and youth makes him slight – a subdued beaten animal of a man – and he is so young it is shocking. And yet how old is he?

Thirty? I watch him for some minutes, time stretched out by recognition. Damn, he's seen me. Hounded, he rises up quickly and leaves the stage.

When I see Doug at the desk I want to capture the moment, to paint it – as Virginia has in her design – after Goya. The level of despair was so arresting, touching and repellent at the same time. I wanted to go and talk to him but this would only mean we would end up in some absurd position. He could not show himself to me any more than he already had. The young man would have to defend himself from my interest. If I were the theatre photographer I might have been lucky enough to capture the image.

I am able to see this image clearly but am outside it and I cannot penetrate. We have no direct contact with our world. Only the sense of a thing, not the thing in itself. I remember why I wanted to direct the play. It tries to speak of what cannot be spoken about, not directly, not at all. Everything is just outside our grasp and we have to learn to accept and be practical about our sense of being outside ourselves. Otherwise the problem is, ontologically speaking, too large.

I wanted to stand with Sam on the edge and fearlessly look on with him and stand alongside him because I believed that he has his feet as firmly on the ground as possible, as he looks unflinching at our loneliest experiences. I imagine that he is not unafraid but that he is not shaken out of himself when he faces the undeniable absurdity of life and undeniable death. He sees a repetition, which makes it possible to keep up the examination, repeating the musical phrases, until he reaches the granite bottom of realities. In this way he is as much scientist as writer and artist. I am truly hurt and annoyed that he cannot see that I, too, have some depth to my experience. Sam is treating me like an idiot, the same way he is treating the actor George, tarring us both with the same brush.

I know something is indissoluble, the indestructible part of the self. When this is discovered, this living, calm, unsullied presence is a bit of a surprise. A creative movement happens like a satisfying bowel movement, simple, comforting, safe. Once this empty space is found, something new starts to grow into it. It comes out of the unconscious. The energy produces a kind of love, an inviolate energy that radiates well-being and kindness. Krapp seems to be undergoing this bleak cycle of renewal. He does not allow himself to suffer contact, but retreats fully enough to find contact in the self. Or does he? The possibility of re-integration in the play is found in the act of engaging with the text, the play itself. By being able to reflect on the man's state, we have the audacious feeling of transcending it.

This is everyman's song, so everyone can pick up its dissonant tune. The move away from contact with outside existence into the interior shadow of unpleasant realities – failure, ageing, death – goes against the notion of the good in the self. It doesn't stop there. The shadow is also in touch with dangerous animal magic. It may be a beautiful resolute fox, or a vixen capable of cunning, stealing, omnipotence or complaint, murderousness or contempt. I am finding that this bookish musing calms me down somewhat and I sit, my body relaxing for the first time today, watching the empty stage.

Janine, George's wife, comes into the auditorium. She is then on the stage looking for George. She is beautiful even without the transformational lens of the camera. She is always around, getting George's dresser, Jo, to help her. Who could resist her? She and George make a striking couple. They are both larger than life and glamorous. Does Sam think he is much too glamorous for this play? I asked Sam what he was thinking so far, but he just looked perplexed and remained silent. The same cold response I've come to expect.

Janine is no longer there. George comes on to continue the rehearsal and is moving around the desk on the stage checking his props. He is counting the bananas and looking at the tapes. The bananas are a startling yellow, the only visible colour. George settles down for a moment or two and then goes off stage to wait for his cue. He comes on and starts to do the initial silent business of eating the bananas, slipping on one of the skins. I sit smouldering in the darkened auditorium. George is getting ready to listen to the old tapes, in preparation for making a new recording of his life. They are his memoirs. The diary of a failed artist, a person who is continually failing but still attempting to move forward, but who fiercely protects his position of loss as one of triumph. There is no moving forward. The only purpose is entropy and death. And yet he and we must, as Sam insists, fail, fail again, fail better.

I watch George and something starts to shift as my concentration takes hold. The monstrous mood lifts as I start to concentrate on the details of the play and I am now determined to set to work to see where there are disruptions to the flow and coherence of the text.

As George starts to speak, there is a clattering at the back of the theatre. I cannot believe that someone is fiddling around behind me in the dress rehearsal. A rowdy, badly behaved, ill-educated teenage-type audience member, a popcorn-eating, coke-swilling lout in my dress rehearsal! I will not stand for it. I turn to look for my assistant who should be putting a stop to it but find no one either side of me. I am furious. I am going to have to sort this intruder out myself. I rise up, my full twenty foot height. And sprint to the back wall. 'What on earth do you think you're bloody well doing?' I shout. 'Who do you think you are, interrupting the rehearsal?' I ask. 'Can't you see what's going on? Have you no brain?'

Every bit of anger and resentment from the past hours comes out in a torrent, almost knocking over the cleaning lady in front of me. She looks frankly terrified and extremely shaken as I rush towards her before she has any chance to escape. She stands there petrified, holding a mop and bucket. Before she can say anything – I'm not sure that she could have uttered a word – Doris Branch, our housekeeper, has appeared in front of her, bodily protecting her from my towering anger. She is a tiny woman of indeterminate age. Her colourless hair has a suggestion of waves held down firmly with a hair net. I take in her colourless sweater, her neat shapeless skirt and lisle stockings and flat shoes firmly rooted on the ground.

'Peter,' she says slowly and patiently, 'there is no need to talk to any of us like that. We have our jobs to do, just as you do.' I feel all the anger go out of me. It simply drops away. 'You're quite right, Doris.' I say. 'I am sorry if I upset one of your staff. My apologies.'

'Thank you, Peter. Your apology is, of course, accepted.'

Thus said, she takes the lady's arm and gently moves her out of the door at the back of the auditorium. She is right. We all have a job to do, George, the cleaning lady and me. This understanding is always what would bring me through the most tortured situations. You simply keep working and something will happen. You work and wait for resources to come and pray when you have taken a risk and are unsure where and when the inspiration will next surface, that it will do so. In order to overcome shame, and fear of failure, and what is not certain, I had, step by step, to give myself over to the tasks before me. I imagine putting on a half-faced fox mask and a cunning, stealthy presence comes up to meet the thought of the fixed mask. I know its presence can be relied on to carry me through. I also know that my apology to Doris will already be enjoyable gossip backstage, as I have never been known to apologise for outbursts. This, already, gives me some satisfaction.

19. The Flydeck

DOUG THE FLYMAN

The time is endless, and musing is wearying me. I first fell in love at a young age, filling myself with a longing that helped me forget about my mother. My first passionate love was with a teenage girl, much older than me. But I only saw how big and beautiful she was. She had translucent skin and large blue eyes. Huge breasts. I had a series of similar crushes on older girls. Was I replicating a solution connected to my mother? Wasn't she after this kind of thoughtless bliss where nothing could impinge? No, this was normal development. I'm meant to fall in love with girls. I always found someone close by and so I suppose that it is not surprising that eventually I married the girl next door. How cunning is that? Mother thought I was at home. In reality I was far, far away in my mind, yet not free. The trouble is, I was and am still puzzled about my mother's absences. The absences, deep holes inside that have now become my own.

I was a good boy. It wasn't hard for me. I played. I studied. I went through the stages expected of me. I would wake up and I didn't complain or demand anything different. I had interests in sport, history, languages and art. I had friends – still do. I listened to music, and thought about girls and sex. I had a partner as soon as I could, eleven years old, so that I always had someone with me. I developed a sexual life from the age of fourteen, not as unusual as you might think. When I finished school I achieved what I was meant to, the right number and mix of exams. I spent years at art school but never knew quite what I was doing there. On the surface I could read the meaning, but below there was the aching doubt. This hindered me. I was never connected up enough. Nor could I find a reason why it should be so – other than a feeling of lack – deep, heartbreaking feelings. The feeling came out as a simple put down. 'You're ridiculous.' That's all it needed. There was no need to say for instance, 'You're a fake,' or 'You're out of your depth or class.' I could intellectually deny that. I could see that was not true. But the prohibition was much deeper. It did not have to worry about reason, intellect or argument. It was a given. To try and make art was vacuous. I could not get beyond that internal fact. I continued making art built on this precarious foundation.

Up until – when? I did feel the comfort of the days. The predictability of home and work, of the expected rhythms of others, and mine with them; all this brought me comfort. I knew I was not entirely part of this momentum, but I was alongside. A different kind of solace was found in secrets, affairs. Sex was a way to wipe out my sad solitude and I could feel the possibility of fusion. Sex exists, so I exist. Ordinary emotional contact makes me feel so fragile and nervous. No one understands or sees this. This secret sexual obsession speaks about my inner exile and also demonstrates my need to connect completely to other people. I had to wipe myself out in the total absorption of fucking, trying to get rid of myself and trying to get back home. Reading, believing, talking, arguing, exploring, all has something for me but it is shot with anxiety. I tend to feel this anxiety when I'm on my own after being with people. Exploring with women particularly, their bodies, their minds: the charge of it all. I have the strength of my body as well as my desire and am invincible. I have to be in love, to want them, and this keeps me alive. It was a juggle, the not telling, the mind being in a number of places at once. I don't feel good about it, but it could not be helped. It was simply a necessity. Still is, but it is not working so well, and I'm plagued by the blue light, and the total terror and hopelessness that can come with it. From moment to moment I find each association, acquaintance, experience, meaningless and dull. The reassurance of the hours no longer has anything but the deadness of habit.

I did try to make something of painting. I thought it could not match my own seriousness, but really it was devilish doubt that killed it off. I wanted it to be what I had seen on the gallery walls, a place where all aspects of life meet in an absolute synthesis. This would transcend all the doubts, make the world cohere, become one, healed. It always fell so far short of this aim. I failed, and continue to fail.

When Becky came along I felt the tug of her – a child so beautiful, warm, an extraordinary presence pulling me in. I could no longer give myself up to the work. Nor could I give myself up to the child. It was either she or I. That is when I knew that some insane force was working within me. I had to hide away and took my usual route, elaborate plans so that I could escape into warm, welcoming bedrooms. At other times I could drink and smoke myself into drunken timelessness. But I could no longer fantasise about giving myself up to painting. I knew I did not have it in me. It had been false hope. I decided to give up painting; give up my art, but with it went the ambition of a deeper life, of life itself. That does sound pathetic. Even I can see that, but that's how it feels. And it's worse. My child can only inherit this possibility of absence in me. I've nothing good to offer her. I feel despair because I have nothing to offer another, particularly to the one who is most precious to me. And now it has happened again. Another child, another mouth to feed and no goodness to give. I am wretched. I've nothing to offer and yet I have to carry on. What else can I do? Every day is full of this wretched conflict. I can't go on, but I cannot stop. If only I could control the sickening, fearful, dark emptiness and the jeering characters, conflicts and voices, then I could get by. The men in my dream creep into the theatre sound box where my mother is sitting and stab her again and again in the back. Terrified, I could neither move nor shout out.

I'm in and out of sleep, drifting again. My sleep is as alive as my waking. I need waking vigilance to avert disaster. I defend myself by keeping constantly alert. I see myself walking down the lane towards the town. I'm alone and in short trousers, so I'm less than nine years old. There is an old derelict house near the lanes, a narrow space between two houses that leads to a main road. It is a transitional spot between the safe solitude of the lane and the business of the High Street, between dreaming and waking. The old house is out of bounds so the children have had to find a way into it, a loose window at the side coaxed into giving way. Inside is a lost, safe world, confirmed by its strange contents. It's an old storehouse, full of costumes and props. My favourite thing is a giant mushroom, which has been taken out of its box by other kids who got there before me. I find out later that this house and the giant mushroom are the property of the Girl Guides. But now it's a magic island, and I can sit on it, or under it, a king, a god perched above or below the world. I'm invincible and invisible when sitting there and I stay there for long periods, always sad when I realise that I cannot stay there forever. I leave the house and walk into the High Street. I drop down a little way to the church across the road. I wander in the graveyard and wonder where my father is. I don't really want to know. Some older boys see me and they start to follow me and imitate my walk. It seems I have been walking with my hands held out in front of me, balancing. They taunt me and threaten me with their loud coarse voices. I shout back at them. I rise up. They can see how tall I am. They throw stones at me and run off. I find my way to the back of the church and the children's lavatories. I need to pee and I am also curious about the girls' toilet. Their bodies, their secrets, will I find out something about them in there? I'm disappointed. Nothing gives me any clues. There are no urinals. Did I know that? I know they don't have dicks so that makes sense. But nothing else is different. It's just as quiet, cold and as unwelcoming as the boys' next door. It slightly smells of shit and piss. I shudder and walk out of there – and almost take a flying leap. The entrance is blocked by the huge body of Cannon Bert. He grabs hold of what feels like the whole left side of my body and throws me in front of him, pinning me against a wall. He calls me a filthy boy. What do I think I'm doing there? He knows what I'm up to, he says. He's been keeping an eye on me, he says. He knows what is in store for me. I'm a bad one.

I'm the one who has a mark on me and I'm going to hang, mark his words. I'm horrified, petrified, shocked. I manage to summon up all my strength and pull away from him, ducking past him, and run as fast as I can, hearing him shouting abuse behind me. Why does it devastate me so? Can't I see he is a madman? No, you can never be sure at that stage if it's you or them. I feel so mad myself, full of rage, at my own stupidity, and at him. I've continued to find it hard to face the world's cruelty. Slights and injustices wrack me. I cannot bear to be in the wrong. If only I could see it differently, but figures like Bert haunt my inner life. It's getting worse. A new set of characters has entered my mental life and I'm not sure what to make of them; terrorists, bullies, gangs, the expected crowds, but also shaman and holy men and women. I am not sure whom I fear the most.

20. The Theatre Stalls

PETER THE DIRECTOR

I'm pleased to have warded off the worst of myself and am sitting back a tad steadier.

Jerry the lighting director is up-and-down moving the ladders around the stage. Only some of the lights can be adjusted from above. He is intent on giving this minimal lighting the most variety possible. He has worked over two nights, no sleep, just himself and a problem, which he hopes may throw up some new innovation. No one wants to disturb him, while inevitably resenting having to deal with the painstaking, painful slowness this kind of working imposes. He is a pain in the arse. We all know this and love him at the same time.

He can push anyone too far at any point. I just expect it to happen at any time and brace myself to ride it out and not sack him, but he came close to expulsion when he came up to me, practically nose to nose – the bastard's as big as me – and said,

'Well, what are you going to do about him, eh? It's shit and everybody knows it. How is this going to end?'

'You'd better get on with your work and speed up if you don't want to be terminated, you've already extended time.'

By implication I point out how easily I can terminate him. He grunts, leans forward provocatively (I can smell the beer and whiskey), reels back and returns to work.

This particular stage is perfectly proportioned, emphasised by the lone figure giving it scale. There is a sense of the blackness being held in by the sides. The audience can't see the area beyond the stage but can calculate it. People watching, grasp the unseen territory as actors and stagehands come on and off, appearing from and disappearing into the darkness. The extension above the grid is no longer filled with flats that come and go for endless scene changes. It is now an expanding dreamscape, which contains the past and the depth of time, all the wondrous theatrical days and nights. It is full of ghosts. I like to think that the unknown space enhances and deepens the audience's awareness of the expanse of the mind – Krapp's mind, Sam's mind.

Only the grid above has a significant number of lights. The concentrated energy of the main lights are cast over the desk like a boxing ring, but must also reach out at times to accommodate Krapp's meanderings. All the parts are deceptively simple, nothing superfluous or shoddy in conception. The shabbiness is the expression of a life that is worn down, worn out, stripped down to essentials, but still vibrating with black grins and frayed emotions. George was pacing the stage earlier, purposely finding himself in the actual place, not the imagined one of the rehearsal room. As we go through the technical rehearsal we have to stop each time that adjustments are made, mainly to the lighting. Jerry has made the place where he sits up over my head in the circle, his vantage point for the duration of the technical and dress rehearsals – the place from which he runs his campaign.

George the actor performs. As each light needs to follow him, the action stops to accommodate this. Jerry is fanatical about his purpose and I would have nothing less from him. He makes sure the light is on each move so that the actor is always in prime focus, always perfectly lit. This makes the actors stand out in the dark in a curious way, increasing their stature and height: it is miraculous to see. It seems to be taken directly from painting and the plastic arts. This particular set shows the contrast of black to white light to startling effect. Against this background the actor is made into a sculpted figure and so becomes much larger than life.

The first time I saw this happening was in rep'. A Spanish troupe of dancers had come to town. They were small, insignificant-looking people, not striking at all. But once the men and women were in costume and lit by spots in a black empty stage they looked tremendously tall and extraordinarily beautiful. I think I fell in love with theatre at that moment. I know I will never tire of its transformational powers. I crave it.

George goes through the play in the slow motion demanded of him, working out his orientation and moves on the stage as they were designed for him. In this way he is renewing his bounds like ritual vows, making himself secure enough to be able to perform. Each movement through time needs to be so familiar as to be part of his body and breathing – only then is he free to find his range within the bounds of what he has remembered. It is all economy, limits are everywhere to be used to their full extent. I begin to feel some empathy for George. He's a good actor and is working as hard as he can on his own. It is an impossible situation when you feel you are doing your best but are at odds with what others are expecting of you. Sam tried to make him work with a concept he has not been able to grasp, has not been helped to grasp, and he cannot trust that or give up the ways in which he thinks this part should work. We pause again and Jerry moves onto the stage.

I made the mistake of going to the pub with Jerry last night. He bought me a drink and started on about the mines. His father and older brothers all work in the mines and he talks about those heroic generations, while he is glad to be the one who escaped.

'I'm more suited to being a vicar's son,' he says.

Poor bloody vicar, if that were the case; neither severe nor gentle churchmen would find Jerry's honed anarchy palatable. I now remember one of Jerry's earlier rants about how Christians shun anger and see it as evil and bad, thereby losing a lot of conscious drive. The Christian rage, repressed, can rise spectacularly in torture, Inquisition, holy wars, unholy political control, or buggering small boys, etcetera, et- cetera. Conversation last night ranged from the miners' strikes to the return of the Vietnam veterans, to the precarious coalition government, all in extremely simple terms. I just politely drank my beer and listened until I'd drunk up and made my excuses. He has a visual right-brained mind – no gift for analysis. Jerry has no arguments, just black-and-white positions.

But as a lighting man, who at this point is the one who pulls the visual punches, I can forgive him just about anything.

Immersed in the work, there seem to be two sharply defined areas, the drama of the internal world of the play and the drama of the world outside: the Winter of Discontent. The evidence of the turmoil outside is in the rubbish-laden streets and the blackouts at night. People are dying in IRA bomb blasts in the city, and pictures on TV show soldiers returning to America from Saigon, lucky not to be among the tens of thousands dead. Each year has its extraordinary events and this year is no exception. America has openly supported the takeover of democratic Chile and many people will die as a result. All these events in the real world sharpen what we're doing here. The attention to the details of existence in the play is made more important, not less, by the spectacle of life-and-death beyond the theatre. News of the Yom Kippur War make us work harder, rather than distract us. Exploration through fictional lives becomes more pressing as world events affect us. They never seem separate, but part of the same universal energy. Writers absorb the *zeitgeist* with antennae that are simply their own existence. Events will filter through consciousness and will come into the imagination and appear in some form or other; mostly not direct political commentary, more as personal synthesis. Many artists are marked by a lack of political guile. Many creative people know a lot about the political world but they have to keep a part of themselves separate from it in order to enable them to be unconstrained by anything partisan in their art. Facing the human condition is apt to forge an artist with a humanitarian bent. The perfectionism of the artist along with curiosity makes something unbiased and unsentimental.

Sam is extraordinary in this respect. He is most unremitting in his refining of his work. He will listen and allow others to show him where they stand. He will give way – a little – if he can see that it will help the rhythm, not hinder it. But he has also done all the groundwork and has made his plans for the plays and will not be dissuaded from the pauses in the language, or the carefully plotted business of the character.

He looks at existence unflinchingly. He believes we're all cursed by being born, only to discover that we are going to die, and doubly cursed if we deny this. His philosophy is one of acceptance of the unbearable truth of mortality. This seems to have resulted in an acute form of humanising, and he embodies this. Ruthless as an artist, he can be the most generous of persons. He gives much of his money away to writers who need it and ask him for funds – it matters little who they are. He will go to great lengths to provide others, and himself, with a good dinner with a good vintage wine. He is generous with his time and conversation. He can also crucify you if you try to guess him; at one moment the avuncular bloke, so warm and generous, another a sharp and razor-like presence.

One wonders when he gets time to write. There are all kinds of stories about his hospitality, effusiveness with his time, helping others. An ordinary Irishman he met by chance in Paris asked him where he might eat, so Sam took him to his favourite restaurant. Only when the man was back in Dublin, telling the tale of the extraordinary generosity of a fellow Irishman, did he find out who he was. I am extremely unhappy that this production is not making Sam happy. He wanders in and out of the auditorium, abstracted, pained, audibly groaning at times. He seems as perplexed as I am. His work with Anna is deeply engaged – a love match – but it is a new work so there is uncertainty. Virginia has told me how unstable Anna is at moments – frighteningly so. There are fears that she will not make it through the actual performance once she's trapped onstage. Everything is in place for the actors, but time is pressing on us.

I've done all that David would have done. I have tried in this crisis as always to emulate David. I have not implored. I have encouraged, suggested, left acres of space to help George find his way. But the way is blocked and I wish David were here. I feel that he could come up with something to help George and Anna to encourage them. It is terrifying to come to an impasse like this, impossible to say, 'We have reached the end.' We have to go on. There's nothing else to do but wait, even though time is not with us. I feel for those Jewish zealots at the Wailing Wall, waiting for God's sign. I suppose the audience in the previews might goad, silently, like prayer, the performances into action. They will want to get behind the plays. But disappointment and waves of protest in the reviews are unlikely to help us.

George looks powerful and jaded under the lights' decisive handling of his face and body. His face is beautiful, razor sharp – even at a distance. He looks tall and imposing and slightly more battered. He goes through the motions of the play while the technicians work respectfully around him. It is living tableaux in action: tableaux demanding this precise detail. The technicians are artisans at work, filling in the details, the black velour, unyielding to the light, the black paint giving the eye some variation. A slight amount of light makes the doorway to the left – stage right – where it is necessary for Krapp to retrieve his essential props: the reel-to-reel tape recorder, the spools of tape, the ledgers and bottles of wine. The tape recorder and spools carry his younger voice, his memories; each new set of memories criticises and excoriates the old. The ledgers are also part of his memory system – tinderboxes of associations, searched and found in the indexes: links to the past made by tuning in. The wine is necessary in managing the pain when making those fateful connections. His fob watch – kept on his person – reminds us of the effects of time – moving always towards the inevitable end.

I watch as the different perspectives of all who are making the play come together and I marvel at it. This alone should be sufficient, and for the moment it is. It's quite a spectacle. George plays his moves over and over; pauses, thinks and starts again. At any moment a halt is called by Jerry or me, or Virginia, and some other figure will appear and take their time doing the necessary around George – who stays put standing, or sits at the desk, or has a cigarette, handed to him by the stage manager. The call goes up to continue and the cigarette is hastily removed, and the wheels turn. Virginia takes her place, as do Jerry and I. Sam seems to have left again at some point. I didn't notice his going.

I try to take up more consciously the role of David. He used to work with surgeon-like precision, slowly, precisely, his steady hand kind and loving, cutting into the action. He would question until you came up with your own answers. I have taken in his methods – yet I have no sense of him, his view. But perhaps his methods were him. He would walk about drawing on his pipe, certain that if he gave the actors time and stimulus enough through the setting, the actor would, with the help of the text, come through. I can see that George may have taken against the text. If so, it is a fatal mistake, no good can come of it. If George has no belief in the play, as well as no sympathy with me, we will sink.

I glance over to where David would sit, further down in the stalls, smoke gently rising from his seat, occasionally lit from front or behind, purposefully chewing on the pipe. I so wanted his approval. If you could prove to him your belief in the play, you could have it. You had to defend it by your actions. He never held a disaster against you as long as you could take it as far as you felt it would go. We all felt that he would be here forever. He died ten years ago. He is still here. Your head always turns to where he sat when you're in difficulty. It still does.

21. The Flydeck

DOUG THE FLYMAN

Demon or god-like martyred figure? I am unsure which of these is the character in the play? I just know that he scares me. More and more I'm in two worlds. The sun rises and sets; the biological, the environmental, the mechanical, the cultural, all slide from one moment to another. Underneath there is the incessant talk, the world inside with its own script running. Some of these underground histrionics are repetitive and dull. Some are pure horror. I could believe that the stabbing of my mother had taken place in the theatre, my dreaming was so vivid. There is a third, more interesting trail that I call the Mysteries, characters visit me like travelling players, strange people who turn up unexpectedly. Death can be forgotten in this underworld, and successfully ignored because it's timeless. I turn to Gurdjieff, Ouspensky, Jung to try to make sense of this. I wish they could help me but all they say eventually seems so thin and abstract. Remy says that Jung says, our imaginary characters come from our complexes; wishes, longings and desires are condensed into people in our minds. So many words. I need images to help make sense of my feelings. And I have images but they make no sense. I am enthralled but also afraid and I sense danger everywhere, undefined. There are times where I see that this is really inside me, not out there. Then I feel the most fear and panic. It is then that the pain becomes intense.

The most puzzling and terrifying sign is the blue light. I have seen the blue flame coming out of others. They do not see it. That is plain. If I talk about it, they will think I am mad. When I listened to the radio, it, too, was surrounded by the blue light. The sound of the radio was understandably distorted and I can be forgiven for thinking that I heard voices cutting across the transmission that were directed at me. Words came through that had shapes and I felt they had come to guide me. I thought the messages were generated to disclose something about the blue light. Indeed, the blue light itself could be the message. It shines like touch paper. It is the blue of the Bunson burners found in the school lab – a hot, searing flame, a cool colour – but hotter than fire and more dangerous. A man stopped me in the street and told me he could see the blue flame on my shoulder. He said I should seek a healer. I should get rid of it, he said. This has been the only acknowledgement I've received. It confirmed the reality of the blue light.

I'm terrified for the children more than for myself. I might infect them and I'm always completely relieved when there is no sign of the light around Becky. It's agony to know that if it gets them, I can do nothing about it. Sometimes, the thought of them being taken over tortures me so much that I give in and say that it's inevitable. It's a sort of giving up when I find a sense of relief followed by guilt and shame, all of which wracks me equally. I see other people that others don't see, that woman for instance. I wish she would come more often. I feel some good energy from her, even though I am frightened. And the Christ figure seems good but not strong enough to ward off the blue light. The blue fire calls me. It beckons, speaking to me. I don't want to hear what it has to say and I resist it as much as I can by pushing it to the side of my vision, trying to ignore it. I fix on it and try to cast it as far away from myself as possible. I cast it away with my eyes, as if I were throwing it away on a fishing line. In this way, it stays tethered to me.

I long to fill the absence my father left in my mother. I found Linda early, looking at her longingly across playgrounds and roadways, in shops and at school. I was fourteen. She was drawn to my attention and simply stayed close by me when she could without being conspicuous. This was my happiest time. I loved everything about her, her stillness, quiet and young radiance. I thought I was saved. She was my best friend and girlfriend for eight years. She was there for all of my adolescence. When we had to part, I went to art school and she went to university, but I did not think it was for good. How could we have drifted apart? She was the raft in my mind on which I floated. With her available, I could always glide through the turbulence. I thought I could find more, that was the problem, and I paid for that arrogance, and I'm still searching. I've searched so long for the calm that I had with Linda. I gave it away and don't deserve anything.

I have to get back to my painting. I know I can find occasional rafts of calm in the making of pictures. In art school I immersed myself working things out and I did come up with answers. I could look and wait and absorb, and eventually something would come through. I must fight off the sense that making has no value. I should have stayed there and not ignored the possibility of teaching. I've put myself right out on a limb, offending too many people, not only blowing up bridges but whole arterial systems, and cannot get back. I decided to leave with my wife and child and believed that I could make a space in a city big enough for me. In the vast anonymity I could breathe. Away from my mother I can think of her with kindness, miss her and not feel suffocated (it's the same with my wife). Mother needed me to fill her life and now I see that she can do other things. She has someone to be disappointed with, a really nice man who doesn't deserve her half-hidden contempt. She continually moans about him. She is surviving, working in the cake shop, and living a life. How would she take the news of another child? I won't tell her. She need never know. She would not know how to deal with it. It would tear her apart – the split loyalties would be impossible for her. I'm far enough away and nothing has to hurt her. I want a new life, a separate life, and it can be that way. I'll have two lives, one here and one there. Once I sort out the blue light I will be able to look after the children. I have no other choice. The blue light doesn't touch Jesse. She is too practical, always looking ahead, outward. Linda, wherever she is, will never be so polluted. It frightened the shit out of me when it surrounded the Christ figure. I didn't believe in the Devil but it was proof, a demonic image. Does my fear generate it? If that's the case then I can control it. That's the most hopeful thought I've had in days.

I wish I could talk to somebody but it would scare anyone. Best to keep quiet and pray. Did I say that? If I said this to anyone they would definitely think I was nuts. Is it such a bad idea? When I was at college, non-celibacy apart, I did see myself as a modern monk, an aesthete living for my work with the woman I needed in the background. It seemed perfect. I was always surprised when people said I was not doing enough. Couldn't they see I was waiting? It had to arise; there was no forcing it.

I smell smoke. A cigarette. The stagehands must be taking up their places again. Jesse said she thought my ability to smell fire was connected to my dad's death. She assumed he had died in a fire. It linked to my recurring dream, she said. Could it be that literal? The blue light *can't* just be a product of my own consciousness; it is connected to a force outside of me, that's plain. I'm not creating it, it has chosen me. I can't work out what it is saying because it manifests itself so randomly. This shows it's of its own mind. I can see no pattern in it, except that it's attached to a person and can appear at any time. People are obviously not aware of it. I see it attach to other people, not just myself. I said to one woman, 'You should get rid of that demon on your shoulder.' She laughed, saw that I was serious, and turned away.

If my father were here would I tell him? I would not tell my mother.

No, neither of them would accept what I've done. I'm so ashamed. I cannot hide the fact that I'm having another child. I know that my escape route is to make the world right through my work. This is not open to me yet, but I will find a way to do it. I can think about what to make while I'm waiting in the wings. In the endless hours of waiting around I can make myself imagine what I'm to create. I can love the children and being with them will help me to be still. They do not know about death and hurt, and do not hurt anyone with their ignorance. It will be OK as long as I do not infect them with my lack.

I need to open my eyes and feel the world around me. Working things out on my own exhausts me. I need to get out of this place, a dead end. I'll think of Germany last summer, on the beach with my wife. I substitute Jesse for her. The sun is so warm and comfortable and I'm feeling hugely fit from swimming and walking. Speaking German frees my head from the ceaseless dialogues. I have a huge erection and am wondering about getting back to the hotel and the big cool bed. I'm another person, free to be myself. I need a little more sex, and humour, quite a bucketful more. Like Remy and the other men.

The knife drawings are a good start. You can't get a more powerful image than the image of a knife. A knife can be a knife just as a cigar can be a cigar. The knife image is multi-layered. All my feelings draw me to the image. I find it soothes me – to think about the knife and to draw it. No one has said the obvious – sinister – but it is sinister and much more. Friends have said that the drawings are interesting – politely, yes – but the knives *are* interesting and the work with them will grow. I don't have to mull over the symbolism; a waste of time. I will have to get into more material, paint whatever – that's the only way to make it grow. Be patient, no chance of a studio yet.

Could I accept that the blue flame symbolises something for me? I could surmise that the blue flame is a code for the red flame, cooler, more dangerous than the hottest anger. The blue flame seems to appear when I can find no way forward – it must come from the deepest conflict and rage. I do have an urge to fight. I had a vision of fighting with another person afflicted with the blue flame and saw it turn into a red flame, then finally a warm glow that died down and extinguished – so the person was dead! This is no option! It might kill me, or someone else. But imagery might be a way to hold and neutralise it in a picture. I must look for as many ways out as possible.

When I think about Jesse and our small room at the top of the large house, or even my wife saying, 'You're a daft bugger you are, what are you on about, get a grip, man,' then it all starts to subside. I'm in another space in my head and I can see the thoughts about the blue flame and the red flame as more than slightly mad, crazy in fact. I'm surprised that I cannot see it that way once the fear gets going. The fear and panic are around more than not.

Jesse says I should talk more and not get so worried when I'm low. She does not understand quite how bleak it gets inside. I love the way she talks to me, and our time together, and it gives me hope that I will be able to find a way through.

I spent a day with Becky and felt much better. She was so delighted to see me. She kept repeating, 'eat me, eat me,' which made me laugh and laugh. It was so delightful. For a moment I thought that I saw the flame near her and I plunged into despair. 'Daddy, what's wrong, what's wrong?' And it disappeared, and I did feel I had imagined it. Then I met my old college mate and was back in the old days when we worked and drank together. During the banter with him I totally forgot all my agonies. I can do that with Remy, too; he's an interesting guy full of humour and quirky ideas. I just need to keep a hold on this and I'll be OK. I've promised to go to the doctor and I'll do it. It will be OK. It has to be.

I look forward to the comfortable armchair of drawing and painting. What a sea of misunderstanding that phrase has caused! Matisse, Bonnard, van Gogh all could turn the struggle of being with a subject into a material structure, which held all the angst and transformed it into a balm. This is what I believed I was aiming for. But it takes so much time and dedication. I need to worry less about the everyday, about people. I need to make my way to the resolution, which is art – the knife is minimal, powerful and lasting and will help me on my way.

I also have to contend with the immediate problem, the play. How can he think that his play can match my dereliction? I yearn for moments of peace away from the incomprehensible around me. Every new hope is overturned and made as hideous as what came before. The world is full of hatred and terror and I seem to be the only one who truly comprehends this. Just look at the news.

I must move to confront this. I get up and make my way across the bridge. And climb through the door that leads onto the backstage staircase, and make my way past the door to the wardrobe at breakneck speed. I arrive at the hub, having slowed down so that no one will be alarmed by my entrance, and go straight onto the stage and sit at the desk. In the spotlight I feel exposed. I'm not sure what to do next. I start to play with the drawer as if I am there to fix something, some positive purpose. Once I've done this I'm stuck and I sit in a state of complete abjection. I realise that others will start to be aware of me. I feel Peter's eyes on me and I slowly move off the stage and race back up the stairs to the fly deck, the only place I know I'm safe.

I look over and see what is happening. George is on the stage and faintly but distinctly around his head is the blue light. My hair sizzles. I have infected him. I step back and feel a sack underfoot and put it over my head. The smell and dust are chocking me so I concentrate on dealing with this by adjusting my breathing. When I surface, George has no more blue light around him. I sit as far back as is possible, listening to the voices below me.

LATE AFTERNOON

22. The Theatre Stalls

PETER THE DIRECTOR

I'm quite settled now the technical is coming to an end. We are almost finished. Jerry is above me in his makeshift office in the front circle. Virginia is seated a number of rows in front of me. Jane is at the board and the crew are in place. I am supported both above and below in an emotional configuration that nicely suggests a family firm. I always sit in the same seat at the back of the stalls, to my left of those facing me on stage, stage right. If the scene makes its mark here where I sit, it will register everywhere else in the auditorium. The audience, all of whose senses are trained on the stage, will be expecting to be stimulated and prompted into active participation. This is not just a mental and emotional engagement, but a demanding physical one. Live performance, actors' voices, reverberate through the body and, dare I say this, I do dare – the soul. If it does not penetrate the soul then it is poor stuff.

Every part of the theatre lends itself to this back and forth trajectory between performers and audience; the energy that comes into the crowd is metabolised and given back to those on stage. The hard stone the Victorian building is made of makes an arena substantial enough to hold the forces within it. The arrangement of the buttoned, rounded, upholstered seats allows us to lean backward while simultaneously leaning into the ambiance. The curtains over the doors soften any impact from outside the auditorium and the city square beyond. The colour red dominates throughout. Red seats, doors, curtains: the red and the gilt walls help create a blood bond. The scattered rust and gold effects in the decor soften faces or inflame them, dependent on the particular surface tension. We make ourselves as comfortable as possible, rough-rouged and warmed by it. The reflections paint the emotional colour of the crowd. Red is such a splendid colour – sending the mind into a raised flutter.

The arch proscenium is much larger than any cinema screen and creates an enormous window into another world; reflecting the singular experience of each person seated. The illusion of theatre is not pretence, its function is to rework experience and set it out before us so that we can begin to understand better, to see for the first time, to be able to see it at all; life repeated, in different forms, hopefully illuminated, ameliorated a little by being recognisable.

I stumbled on this as a young child. I was given a small toy theatre and found that in the process of making up stories I could articulate my own experience and feelings in a way not at all possible without the story and the lies. You had to be able to tell lies in order to tell the truth. Once you have grasped this, the world can be yours.

As a child I discovered something without having any notion that this knowledge was profound. I could play with an extremely small number of elements and these would be enough to create a much bigger reality. Figures and small objects, or 'props,' would be all that was needed to make a story with characters and meaning. And what's more, it became entertainment, a way of getting through to others, to be liked by them but, more importantly, understood. It was always best when it was about something that truly engaged and moved me – about boys and girls and mummies and daddies. Upsets and crashes and secrets and imagined scenarios that I had witnessed at home or at school or out in the town. Stories were important, especially if one's own scenarios could be identified, overlaid or inserted.

Make-believe is a place where happenings and feelings can be placed at a remove and examined without being too raw or too explicit. When I came out of the National Service, I found myself playing again, in a real theatre. This helped me to keep sane when I was uncertain of who or what I was. As a little boy, with my puppets, I put my hands and heart through the tiny toy arch and then as a man walked through the grand scale proscenium and found a space for all the processing I needed. It's a great mistake to clutter up the stage. If you start to build elaborate detailed structures the eye and mind will be excited but will soon tire because there will be nowhere to exercise the imagination. The task is to have a few bits and pieces, as few as possible in the frame, to allow for the words and story, the actors and the people watching. Only then can there be an optimal exchange. To have nothing: no set, no props, no costumes, wouldn't work either. The actors need objects to allow them to interact with ordinary things, to help them find responses within themselves.

But you have to know the parameters of the setting before you set foot in the rehearsal room. The rehearsals have to plot towards a completely thought-out space – not an imaginary one. So Virginia, Sam and I work out the space before anything else. Actors are cast, readings are done, but at the early stage, in the first days and weeks, sometimes months, the staging and planning precede this. I wish I were back in those earlier days at this moment with hindsight to guide me, when we were at the stage of the creation of the world of the play. Virginia is the person who makes this possible. No one can underestimate her role in the first phase. She is God's architect who makes the descriptions in the play into actual physical space. I, too, hoped be a great creator, the godlike director for a time. The set builders too have their moment: a rabble chorus. Finally it should be the actors who are in ascendancy, and the writer will be recognised once his writing has been realised from actual stuff.

David said that this theatre must be a place for actors and text. He reacted against the staleness of the type of theatre he inherited, which was baroque, overtly realistic old-fashioned sets and old writing, as well as classical writing, which is not the same thing. He introduced new writing and allowed actors to discover it with the playwright. But at the beginning, the director and designer do need to have their time and behave as gods and mythical creatures have always behaved. They lay foundations, so the important work can take place. Without the structure, all would be too loose, a raggedy mayhem, like a continuous read through – fun but only a tiny, yet lively indication of what could be possible. So, at last, after weeks of rehearsals in empty rooms with plans taped on the floor, we are ready.

All of us who worked during the war understood the use of scarcity and limits. The war, and the paucity of being artists taught the gift of economy, so useful to the inventiveness, inspiration, ingenuity and originality of production. Limits force new solutions and it is good to be reminded about the ability of the mind to respond to a lack and find another way. George is younger, part of a newer, more hopeful generation, one that expects to be given their head to find new solutions. Does he feel we are not giving him a chance to bring something new to the piece? I have been lucky to be part of so many demands for new solutions, and to be encouraged to think that I could find the answers. That makes me one of the luckiest buggers on the planet. I only hope it continues. I'm sorry Sam has not given me more credibility in this regard. But he is smitten with Anna. He has seen her as an extension of what he is doing and can't let go of her. I have felt enraged by their excluding me, I see that now. But Anna cleverly gives me the odd hint that she is protecting me, guarding me from Sam's extreme need and dealing with it herself. So can I just accept that this humiliation has happened? Being marginalised as the director of half of the production?

It is striking that so much can happen in the monochrome picture in front of me. The grubby white shirt is a smallish mass of white and shadow. The surface blacks of Krapp's coat, waistcoat and striped trousers undulate as he moves around, the movement of light making a subtle pleasing texture, a black sea creature (a bottom feeder) moving in blackened night water. The yellow of the banana is a thrilling shock if you're near the stage, only slightly less so in the back stalls. Krapp's hair is a curly slightly greasy mass, the boots caricatured, too large clownish shapes making a mark of their own: all so sparse and yet so rich, so beguiling, as you find yourself able to apprehend each sign and allow your feelings and mind to roam around them.

White light contains the whole colour spectrum so that any colour or change of surface, however small or discreet, will work with it. Even the blue-black ledgers give off enough coloured light to make a connection. Someone would resonate on stage with the discoloration, the injury, like the sensitised watcher settling down to absorb every nuance of the visual realm and action.

The audience will be made to engage in a different way with these plays, which make an essential demand of them. The style taxes the audience, but it doesn't tire the mind, nor fatigue their hearts. As Sam has stated, it is a blood fatigue. It exhausts but does not stupefy.

Is George afraid that he will stupefy the audience? That the words will not engage the audience and they won't be with him? The works will make the writer's demands of the audience, but perhaps George is uncertain they will be able to move into their own associations, into their own responses. Or perhaps he does understand this and feels it will have little to do with him? The play is conceived as a musical production and it is the actor's task to play it as conducted, but I can almost sympathise if he does not want to do this. Yet I need to help him see that it could work for him.

He would be wrong to feel this exclusion. He is part of some bigger communication. Without the narrative frame there is a challenge put to the audience by the writer. The encounter with the writer is a relationship, a separate relationship to that of actor and audience. Sam is free to antagonise and even punish his audience and he counts on their willingness to deal with their frustration.

23. Outside

VIRGINIA THE DESIGNER

Why wait and muse? The lack of too much to do at this stage is leading thought in unexpected directions. I wonder if I could slip home for a while, now that the theatre has emptied and the curtain has been dropped. The curtain coming in signals that all the preparation for the dress rehearsal is in place. The stage is set. I decide instead to go upstairs and see how things are backstage with the actors and the wardrobe. I can walk through the door hidden at the side behind a curtain, but I walk to the back of the auditorium and head for the canal. It is a perfect, bright sunny day.

The pavements buzz with the workday crowd: workers, shoppers, tourists. It is slightly breezy, the tall old trees and buildings light-hearted, open, free. Dufy comes to mind. The scene is lightly drawn with a free hand. I sit on the steps and have a cigarette. Some of the company is drifting back to the stage door from the pub and each one acknowledges me in some way as they pass. I decide again to go upstairs, and make my way down the small side alley. I feel light, part of the lively sketch of the city streets. I am one of the drawn characters, a woman in artist's clothes, paint-stained, hair tied up, putting out a cigarette. A rat disappears behind the bins, a comic note in the street scene. It is rather fat. It can't be feeding on the theatre bins, must be the restaurants nearby.

I walk straight past the stage door man, Stan, and up the stairs leading to the dressing rooms. The earlier commotion, after the burglary, has died down. The calls that go for the half hour before the dress rehearsal are some time off. Then, unexpected, comes a more urgent call, asking for the whole company to come downstairs. I wonder what can have prompted it and turn back down the stairs.

We are not an enormous company, two actors and the crews, but we seem to fill up the space behind the prompt desk. Then I feel the water under my feet. What on earth has happened? I push my way forward onto the stage. The working lights are on and the water is dripping everywhere. It leaks out of the walls and drips from the ceiling thirty feet above. Jesse thunders past me.

'What idiot did this?'

She looks stunned for a moment then turns to me decisively. 'We'll need to bring down all the material we can – the blacks?' I ask her if there are any curtains in the store upstairs. 'Yes, we have loads.'

'Let's go for those,' I say. Everyone follows us up the stairs and soon we are coming down loaded with armfuls of curtains and drapes. 'I wish we had the material from The Sea,' says Jesse. 'I hated sewing up all those blue bales of cloth. It would be my revenge.'

It takes a few moments on the stage to realise what has happened. Water has cascaded down because someone has pulled at the fire sprinklers by mistake. I have never seen the sprinklers in action and am impressed by the amount of water involved. The stage is truly flooded, everything soaked. While all hands are on deck mopping up, the lighting crew is all over the stage trying to assess the danger and damage.

Jesse tells me the story in hushed tones as we work. Remy, a newish stagehand, keen and wanting to show initiative, knew that the first task was to raise the curtain. The pulley for the fire sprinkler is right next to the pulley for the iron curtain. He pulled the fire sprinklers by mistake. He was mortified, says Jesse, looking at me to see if she could gauge the severity of my reaction. He is certainly very red in the face. He stands out, a beacon of discomfort and shame, one amongst the labourers stuck into clearing up his mess. Of course I know who Remy is. He is the one hoping to study psychology. He does not miss the chance to share his reading, particularly on Jung. He threatens to become a Jung bore, a worse crime than causing a deluge.

Peter returns in the middle of the cleaning up. I can see that he is holding himself back and am wondering if his frustrations with the rehearsals will find a target in this hapless boy who looks barely twenty – although Jesse tells me he is older. Jesse says he has left a job in the city. He had been offered a place at university and so far turned it down. He does not know what to do next. I sit in the stalls to scan for damage and problems. Jerry, the lighting director, approaches me and assures me that we can go ahead even though the water comes in above the stage lighting bars. He goes over to talk to Peter who is on the opposite side of the auditorium. I am instinctively staying clear of him for the moment.

These kind of practical problems are a nuisance but they are always the easiest to solve, unlike sticky creative conflicts. 'Spilt milk' is soaked up so we can carry on with the more complex tasks. Remy is probably expecting to be sacked, having come from the city. But I am not so certain that will happen. Environmental hitches are not a hanging offence in the theatre. 'He would be sacked in industry,' the stage door man confirms for me as I pass him going back and forth, checking on various responsibilities.

Once the mopping up is finished, and it happens fast, I sit back and marvel at the transformation made by the water. There is a definite subterranean dankness. The theatre takes on the feel of an enormous, dark, damp cave or pitch under rocks and trees. A confirmation of the damp, an additional stage sound, comes from constant slow drops. The water continues to let me know it is there by slow drips descending from up on high catching the light and gently landing on the stage, luckily mostly at the sides. The stage has come alive and is weeping. David's ashes should have been painted into the fabric of the walls, not some unlikely place in the countryside.

I hope it will not disturb the actors. They have enough to manage. I wish they could enjoy a new element they can weave into the drama, an amusing improvisational presence. In fact I doubt if they will notice. For me the weeping would be a welcomed counterpoint, in defiance of what might be a farcical calamity, not the wished for comic tragedy. There is nothing to lighten the mood here and no happy ending in sight.

THE DRESS REHEARSAL

24. On Stage

SAM THE PLAYWRIGHT

Reaching the auditorium, jumping from the side of the stage, the dress rehearsal is about to start.

'Ah, Sam,' says Peter, surprised by my appearance.

People are relaxed, standing around, as everything is ready: nothing to do but wait. Bodies hanging there in suspended outline. Having been propelled down the stairs by my agitated state, I now find myself suspended with them. This is not unlike the state I was in upstairs but I'm now less cut off from the anger I feel about the play. It is so lacking in its essential energy, so laboured and earnest and not right, tight-arsed like someone walking around trying to hold a fart but failing to stem the bad smell. For all the apparent ease, the air is stale: Bedlam's bedroom late at night. The mood between the key players is fetid with constipated emotion, nothing flowing. I can feel the danger of getting caught up in the contaminated atmosphere and have an urge to run away out into the street.

I step back. The scene seems calm enough but everyone's hit a low point: George on stage in his costume, the director and designer sitting quietly in the stalls, the technicians hanging around. No more preparing, everything laid out ready for the off. People hope they're prepared enough.

Nevertheless, sitting looking at the magnificent stage with the small group of people placed in and around it, it would be hard for a casual observer to see anything other than an absorbing picture. No bright lights disturb the blackness of the set. The working lights leave it flat and sparse, making George a shadowy figure, hard to read. He gets up and potters around aimlessly, stretching a little and pulling at his clothes. He then pushes himself this way and that, gently. His movements are precise, stretching his muscles and skin. He scratches his head and taps his foot noiselessly on the floor. The stage manager walks onto the stage and past him, and he smiles at her. The movement is slow and in my mind it is slower. The flat working lights allow me to see the figure standing up in the flies above. He is also poised, only moving slightly, as if adjusting his balance or adjusting a cleat as a gesture of readiness. The movement is not enough to test the cleat's safety but it lets the body have an outlet for a mood that is hidden and waiting; waiting there to be forced out into the open if it is to be known at all.

The work that has gone into it! Peter and Virginia are sitting a little way off from me. He is reading – the script? Doubtful. She looks quietly straight ahead. He asks her something and she readily replies. She is contained. She knows she can be relied upon to be steady. She has done all she can to enhance the play and the performances with her designs and costumes, and her attention to everyone and every detail. She must be feeling some of my disappointment with the man's performance. There's no outward sign of the stalemate between the two men sitting except some marked distance from each other. Their eyes never meet. Since arriving at the theatre, the very place where things can be seen to take a final shape, despair has set in. I can't see this final rehearsal pulling them out of it. They are so mistuned to the play. Who could have predicted it? They're both trying to hide the shame of disappointment. I have never seen the play have this deadening effect on a whole company before. They are doubtless blaming each other for their own disaffections. They would clearly like to shit on each other. It would be dangerous to come between them, like putting your head down a toilet. For a moment I see the two figures lit in such a way as to pick out their big heads and make them stand out from the others around them. Then the unspoken stand-off is clearer. Neither is going to give way because they have no idea what to do. The other minor characters in the scene are affected by it, laid low by their unhappy disaffection, infected by the drab conflict. Nothing they can do either.

Jesse appears on the stage, a moment of light relief and comedy. It's obvious from her faltering gait that she has no purpose there. She comes on and goes off, pretending to have some last minute work to do. She looks at George as if she's sizing him up – for a fitting. At this stage? I see Virginia is alerted to her. What is she doing? Looking for that boyfriend of hers, drawn towards him, drawn by a terrible heat – the pull of the promise of hotheaded rapture. She is wearing a long pinkish dress, not bright, but a slip of bright-jeweled silky cotton topped with her hennaed hair. Her high espadrilles make her teeter a little (she and Janet both have this balancing act in common). Her posture and purpose are unsteady. She moves off the stage, ungainly but bravely trying to look, against the odds, that she is meant to be there. She is a flash of painted colour – one of a colourist's masterstrokes, like Matisse's goldfishes, but more pinky red and less graceful. She has the potential to be a Modigliani figure, an etiolated femininity, but she blows it, her possible elegance clumsily undermined by her distorted purpose. She has slightly bad posture. She hurries off stage left and I sense her standing in the wings, looking up at the flies above. She and her man are undone by the undeniable, sexual urge that is such a messy business and cause of so much humiliation and pain. The play could do with some of this energy, the unsightly distortion brought about by libidinal energies.

The urge to act arises. I have had my cue. It has nothing directly to do with the impish Jesse. I would have made it without her. There are still a few moments. I need the time, just a few seconds to gather myself again. I thought I had long ago gotten past the milestone of lethargy and procrastination, but at this juncture I still have it within me. Jesse's flash of colour is gone, the tense scene returns. My characters are still in place, too self-absorbed to be ruffled by the moment's disturbance. I look at the picture so far created: the dark interior, the still single figure, the others all separate and distant. There is an air of loss and separation. The men are forlorn and angry, the women patient and loyal. The flats and the entrances and exits to the stage and auditorium suggest others waiting and watching in the wings. The main characters at the moment are the director and the Actor King, who have nothing to do with my character. I need to get him back into the space, right into the centre, its heart. I have to take back what is mine and not let them destroy it with their resistance. Am I in danger of destroying the play? I don't think so. Would it crush George? I need to rescue him as he is in an ignominious position. My man Krapp needs to be rescued from shame. He is not shame. He is the opposite. He is a walking, living shadow. I can see him so clearly. He's in my body contours and I can project him onto the stage like a lantern image or a hologram. I need to flesh him out, and my mind and body work at the speed of light as the mask of Krapp takes hold. The urge gets strong enough for me to see clearly what I am going to do. I do not hesitate. If I allow for any distraction, think about it in any other way, I might miss my best chance.

I find myself on the stage wishing George a good day, asking him how he is, and would he mind if I just demonstrate something to him about the play. I said that after the last run through I had thought it was not quite what I had in mind, and could I show them what I did have in mind? I don't give him time to answer. He is a little taken aback, I can see, and I hear a rustling in the stalls. But my resolve is strong and I stand there as if what is going to happen is the most natural thing in the world – the only thing to happen – the only thing to expect. It was always going to occur. I am taking my raincoat and suit jacket off.

'This is more what I had in mind,' I find myself repeating.

I ask George if I can borrow his waistcoat. I will need the pockets. He takes it off slowly and hands it to me. I ask him to take a seat in the auditorium for a moment and he looks as if he may step down. I put the waistcoat on. It fits over my white shirt, which is far too clean, but OK for a rehearsal. I walk around the stage and I am older, unsteady on my feet, short-sighted, hard of hearing. I know my voice is cracked with a distinct intonation. I am slipping into something, a small but a substantial part of myself. It is almost another skin but mine all the same. It is a relief to sit at the desk and check that all the props are where I left them. I start to fumble in my pocket. George takes the hint and hands me an envelope, a fob watch and a bunch of keys. He stands back, way back to the side of the stage. Jane is beside me. I tell her to start the rehearsal. She seems not to understand but obeys me and goes off to start the cues. The curtains are drawn. George is now on the other side of the curtain. The working lights dim and the room light above me is off. I'm surrounded by darkness.

The curtain rises. The lights come up. I put the envelope in my pocket, look at the watch – it is time – I take out my keys. I squint at the keys on the ring and choose the key that I want. I am excited as I move around to the front of the desk and unlock the drawer. I peer and feel inside the drawer until I find a tape. It's not the one I want so I put it back and lock the drawer. In anticipation I unlock the second drawer, feeling inside, I find a large banana. I can feel its yellowness. It is so smooth yet acid yellow to the touch. I am surprised at how erotic it feels, an extension of my body. Its contour is both in my mind and in my hand, like holding my own penis. I lock the drawer and take my prize to the edge of the stage. I stroke the banana, peel it and drop the skin at my feet. The banana placed in my mouth is a drug, soothing and mild, its pale yellow flesh like slightly sweet milk. I could stay there poised forever, but I break my mood by biting into it. I pace to and fro, reminding myself that I should be meditatively eating a banana. I speak the instructions inside my head, lovingly repeating them to myself. The times I have read those instructions! The times actors have also read them and followed them, knowing the score. I will not let them down. Another part of my attention keeps an inner eye on the dropped banana skin. I am able to slip upon it, and to ski while waiting to facilitate my large faux fall. I enjoy saving myself. I have avoided ignominy and death. I look down at the conquered skin and push it over the edge of the stage. Triumphant I keep pacing and relishing my banana, eat it all up.

I repeat this whole sequence again, drawer, banana, stroking, eating, pacing, but this time I do not fall, I simply throw the skin into the pit. I have only eaten half of the second banana, which I hold sensually in my mouth. It is cool and organic in this dark colourless place. I am holding a mute, sensual, piece of flesh. But I must get on, so it is placed in my pocket.

Speeded up by my bold actions and adrenalin I rush to the back of the stage, disappearing through the door in the flat. I am amazed by my energy. The stage manager Ruth is waiting for me, wide-eyed in the dark. She listens with me to the sound cues, the popping of the corks. We breathe staring at each other, her eyes exceptionally wide. Ruth hands me the prop ledger and I burst back onto the stage, blasted with light.

The ledger is a nice weight and I put it down respectfully on the desk. I feel the smear of banana on my face. Rubbing my mouth and wiping my hands on George's coat, I feel an unexpected joy. I am safely back inside myself – and beside myself with pleasure. The glee moves into an exaggerated rubbing of hands. I open the ledger and start to look for the reference I need, the box and the tape number. Long-remembered words spill out of me as I search for the imaginary record.

Oh, the joy of the words. The joy of searching for the old recording, my younger self: I know exactly the one I am looking for. The tapes have their own personalities, own selves. Putting my hand on the tape, I want to feel gold. I find it. 'Spooool.' And load it into the machine, my hands rubbing again. I look down at the notes made for this recording and read them out to myself, pouring over the words, letting them stir images in my mind. Feelings and images start to surface. My happiness slowly recedes but not my relish for the past. Key words stand out and demand a link with the present. Some references mystify me, including. Then 'Farewell,' turning the page, 'to love'...' My heart stops.

I put the ledger down and am now gripped as I move forward to turn on the tape, the cue for sound. Jane does not let me down. The sound fills the theatre. It is George's voice that I hear on the tape. It is not my own but I accept it as the voice of a much younger self, my character at the age of thirty-nine. Sitting on the stage at sixty-nine I am the same age as Krapp. I am Krapp. The words of the play roll out of the machine. They are not part of me, not memory, but a former self. Momentarily I see my small audience: an electric current between us. I am plugged in. I hear, 'Thirty-nine today.'

I am startled by the volume and clarity, disturbed by the voice that is I but not me. I move to settle down to listen to the tape, which plays on. In doing so I knock over one of the boxes. Rage sweeps through me. To hell with the other recordings, I'll have none of them. I switch the tape off and sweep another of the boxes and the ledger onto the ground. This makes me feel powerful, my drives humming. I switch back on and hear a voice at my peak. As I listen, busy with myself, I am taken with the volume of my younger voice as it projects out into the darkness. I hear I've spent my birthday drinking wine alone in a public house. Now I am back home and glad to be back in my own rags.

The light in the room is hung in the centre where it creates a pool of light. This makes me feel less lonely. It makes me happy that I can go in and out of the light. It is a great comfort that I can exist on either side. I know the devil is beside me in the darkness yet I am nevertheless otherwise content with myself because I have managed to look at the devil in the dark and lived to tell the tale. There are grains of crystal in my life that are unique, nothing can reduce or destroy them. I have separated the light from the dark so they can exist together. Old Nick is here with me, aware of what is going on. Reason needs to separate body and mind, death and life. Allowing both to exist is a transgression. I was punished for this for a long time, as Krapp has been punished. Krapp still has a desire to mingle light and dark to promote the union of the gross body and undeniable spirit. The bringing together of black and white is still in him, and here with me now. The essential self keeps in with the light, only if it keeps close to the darkness. This essential light is there even though I am a dirty old man befuddled by drink; my poetry still intact, but much harsher, sardonic, simpler.

The play is being acted by me but I am no longer aware that I am a player. The play is playing me and I am not even conscious of what I am doing or saying. The action streams out through me from a well inside. Yet moments stand out and I can watch myself.

I barely recognize myself in Krapp's pompous, even tone, his assured narrative pace.

My thirty-nine year old self is distracting himself by randomly thinking out loud on the tape of old Mrs McGlome, who would always sing songs of her girlhood at this hour. Could I? Could he sing? He asks myself. No (forcefully), I never sing, he says. I know later that I will have to contradict him and break into a hymn. My feelings for him as I listen intently are mixed. I am drawn to him. I admire him, yet I find him repulsive, unlikeable.

When did I have this notion, to record myself, year after year on my birthday? Little did I realise how extraordinary these recordings would become as the years stretched between them. The connection between my different selves is tenuous and contradictory.

I listen to George's talk about a tape made years earlier when we were in our twenties. He, the young Krapp, is glad to wish the old misery of first loves away. Remembering a moment of the pure beauty of Bianca's eyes he is wretched, there is no way he can feel part of her or close to her and he has to give her up. He says he is glad to do it but you can feel the false bravado. I am shaken. And the memory of a saddened girl in a railway station in a shabby green coat. Heartbreaking misery. Quite right! In my twenties he, I, am giving up on this hopeless pursuit of happiness. And I had lost our beloved father. It is so long ago but the pain still cuts through. I am scoured when faced with my old selves. They burn, branding me.

Listening to the aspirations and resolutions of our twenties, George and I have a chance to laugh out loud together. I am particularly amused by his determination to drink less. Would I really have liked to have been the kind of man who did not drink to numb the pain? I don't think so. What, and miss out on that brand of spirited exuberance helping the loosening of the brain? Anyway, the anti-hero's soul is made of iron spirit, not diluted with coppery soft drink. If I am to be able to endure reality I must, for God's sake, have a proper drink!

The youngest of us, thinking of his Opus Magnus, calls out for the care of God as he evokes Providence. Unexpected that. I, Krapp who is sitting on the stage, breaks into a hymn.

'Now the day is over
Night is drawing nigh---igh,
Shadow---s'

The earlier revelations are matched now with new, almost identical grooves, different overlays, a receding mirror, but every image a variant, unique, its own revelatory time. The images recede through time and mutate into the future.

Krapp is ever evolving. He does not want to relive past experiences, or satisfy earlier desires. He has taken on the constancy of change, and weathered catastrophe and disruption. He knows his equilibrium can be punctured at any minute by catastrophic panic, hence the need for drink. He still has no choice but to move from anticipation to disappointment, on and on. I had to make George suffer, as endurance of failure is a precondition of this play.

I have to switch off. I look at my watch and get up to go backstage. Jane, bless her, is waiting. I need a breather. Each ten seconds we hear the sound (recorded) of the pop of corks. She hands me a glass of water and I take a short draft. I am coughing as I come back in. I sit down and listen with an assured train of concentration that allows for varied levels of thought. I realise now why I had taken out the purple drinker's nose from the original drawings of Krapp. It was too obvious, as is that damned hymn.

I'm still in the player's zone and am back with the tape booming around me. A mother's death: the image of a black crow in widow's dress. The pain of widowhood borne too long. It, too, is heartbreaking. I love my own words. They do not belong to me and yet they are mine. I switch off and reach for the dictionary. Uncertain in my mind about whether the word viduity has been used in the past. A widow is in a state of grace; a place of pure pain and loss which is the true condition. It is so stark, clear bright, that knowledge of loneliness, belonging to me and to Virginia, who I know is now watching me (I hope with some enjoyment). We all long to be gone when we are in such pain.

There is a wait outside her window, wanting her, my mother the widow, to die and to see the blind drawn down. As I wait for her death there is a comic encounter with a buxom nanny and a huge pram. She is voluptuous and emits sexual signals but threatens to call the police when I venture to talk to her. Sexual comedy dances beneath death's window. But her black eyes, 'like crysolite', are the heralds of death.

And the reference to the black ball: I was playing with a white dog, throwing the black ball, it was in my hand, as the death blind was pulled down. Something fuses in the synapses. I gave the ball away to the animal but the ball in my hand is forever scorched into the palm, the gesture of sacrificing sense to spirit.

This year of the death of our mother was a spiritual one of storm and vision. The vision is a terrifying one but it contains fire and granite and exposes something unshatterable in the self. At thirty-nine I am describing how I propose to bring together darkness and light, and I cannot bear him being so vocal and explicit and pompous about his aesthetic illumination. I am disgusted and shut off the tape and wind it forward. I can't bear it, curse at his verbosity and turn him off and wind on again.

I find I had accidently moved from intellectual revelation to the encounter with another lover, the moment of impossible longing lying together in a small boat. We had silently agreed we could not be together and yet clung together lying in the punt. She is so wanted but so alien and so feared. The need to enter her, to know her body and soul feels so completely impossible. I listen for what seems endless time to the minute descriptions of our last time together, to each completely other, separate, alone. But I am really stuck with the vision of her breasts.

The images in the play astound and move me. They are my life, my character's life, all life. I pause the tape at my cue. I switch off the tape and brood over what I have heard. I go through my character's rituals. The banana is soft as I take it out of my pocket. The envelope is there as well as my watch. The envelope contains the thoughts for the new tape. I put the objects back in my pocket.

Back offstage, I am faced with Jane and more stage sounds, this time the clinking of the bottle and glass. I am unsteady as I go back onstage – rocked by my own revelations. I'm ready to go through with the recording. I fumble in the drawers and take out a new reel and place the tape in the machine. I switch it on. I talk again to myself. I switch it off. I then talk again and realise that I am switched off, so I switch the tape on. I laugh inwardly at the tragic-comedy, the merry-go-round.

The bitterness about the long wait for publication breaks through, so do the images of other lost loves and the whorehouse. I'm now maudlin and telling myself to go to bed. Images of Christmas and Sunday mornings in Ireland! Ah, that old misery...

It's definitely getting near the end. I wrench out the new tape and throw it away; put on the old one, and repeat the passage in the punt.

Here I end this reel. I sit motionless, deeply moved. And the tape whirrs on in the silence.

The audience is silent, reverent. Then the small group is rushing up towards me, smiling and hesitant all at once. George looks unreadable. He may have been able to see something. I hope so. Virginia says nothing but looks at me with great love and fondness. It is important to love this part of us, the shame, the humiliation, the loathing, the shadow. Only then can we live.

It feels as though I have been on the stage for only a few minutes, but all the same, a very long time. A sportsman completely caught up in my game, I have been in a different space and time, my own small realm.

I am done, nothing more to do now and nothing more to add. The others must start again. They are already beginning to reset the stage. George has thanked me, cursorily I think, no real hint of warmth and he has gone off to his dressing room. At the end of a rehearsal period, coming in to the theatre, all the cast have a dressing room, the director has his office. I have nowhere to go. I think of going back upstairs, but no. My time is finished here. There's nothing more to do, only to take my leave. I gather up my clothes, put them on and head outside. Only then do I remember the second play and realise that I have to stay. So I turn back to the wardrobe.

25. The Fly Deck

DOUG THE FLYMAN

I need to slip away. The threat is too great. There is a blue fire consuming me and I cannot extinguish it. It is threatening everyone and I am the source. I thought I could keep going but I can't. I cannot go on with the fear, pain and separateness. The world is an empty place. There is nothing I can connect to that would make me feel differently. I am on my own and people are saying they are there but it is not true, I am utterly alone and this cannot change. I had hoped I could keep going for them, to keep up the lie of existence, but I am disappearing into a tunnel, which is leading me to where I have to go. This has to be for the best. They will cry, but they will understand that I am no good for them. I will contaminate them with the blue light. There is only one solution – the only thing to be done now. It is the moral thing to do in the circumstances. Sam would understand this. He would agree I have the right to do this. I have to act while I have the courage. If I hesitate, the opportunity will be lost. I need to focus. The ropes are here to help me. I have thought about the distance needed. I would prefer that it was a complete disconnection of the head from the body. I have thought about how I would get my head off. How I would disconnect my head from my spine. How far I would have to drop. These plans I have kept in reserve for a longtime. They may seem macabre but they have been my balm. The physical pain will release me from the hell I am in now. I am not going to throw myself off the fly deck, that would be too dramatic and I would need twice my height in rope. No I will stay on the deck and hang from a cleat. I reckon I will need a five-foot rope as I am six foot one. That is the drop and that is perfectly possible here. But I don't want them to see me. I may disgrace myself, piss myself, I would rather that was out of sight. But I think I can bear the strangulation as I have a high pain threshold. I once walked for two hours on a splintered leg. I just said to myself 'another ten minutes' and thought no further. This will be much swifter, as the increments will be much shorter. It has to be rope, to be strong enough. I am surrounded by rope. If I cannot separate my head from my spine, then I will have to face the pain of strangulation and asphyxiation. I am ready to do this. I am already feeling better. I am about to be free. I just need to keep working out what to do. The knot needs to go to the side, beneath the ear, on the ear. I can picture a noose I have drawn in the past. I will have to hold it to see how it will fall. The setting out point *is* important. Where to kick off? There are so many moments that have shown the way, tightening and the tension that shows where the weight is being held: gravity will do the work for me. All I need to do is jump. In the tightening of the watchstrap or the shoelaces, and a necktie of course. The simple slipknot is all that is needed. How to tie the noose? The rope is allowed to hang down and then a length is brought back on itself to make the slipknot. It is as simple as that. Make a bow, then up to the top, then it goes around itself. From the top or the bottom? No, I am making it too complicated. Just create a loop and tie it and thread the rope through the loop. It will work. You see it everywhere. When you are out climbing you throw an anchored rope over a wall and you pull on it and it makes a grab. The same when you tether a boat. Pulling on a lead or a rein, for a dog or a horse, they all have the same purpose, to hold the weight. But the cleat I am looking at above me will only hold for strangulation. This garroting will not be so pleasant. I will have to hope it will be enough. I am usually able to judge these things. I think of the ends, the executions of the James Gang, Billy the Kid and Dick Turpin. As a boy I always thought they had heroic ends. My childhood heroes.

 I jump.

 And now I am floating high above the stage and I can see everyone below me, not just on the stage but in each place in the building. Jesse is sitting at her machine. Janet is in the office. George is on the stage, and Jane is separated from him by the stage flats reaching up to me from the set. In the auditorium sit Virginia, Peter and Sam, with Jerry sitting up above them, sitting with some of the stagehands. I can't see Remy among them. I am flying too high for them to see me. I see George performing but I cannot hear him, which is a blessing. But then he changes and I think I am seeing myself down there, and then Sam in the actor's place on stage. I hear a crash, a thud, reverberating through the building, as if some huge truck has crashed into it. I must float down and see what is happening. Maybe the company is in danger?

I hear a voice. It is Remy shouting my name. 'Doug, Doug!! Can you hear me?' It is as if he is shouting in my ear. I can feel my face being slapped and my chest being pounded. The pain is terrible, my throat and neck are burning up. I can hear Remy's voice again. 'Help me,' he cries out loud, 'call 999.' The intensity of the pain in my head and throat is increasing and I am alive.

26. Postscript

VIRGINIA THE DESIGNER

Dear Peter,

When I heard the shocking news at the theatre, I had to go out and walk around the block. I am not sure how long I walked. It must have been two or three times round. News comes of others all the time, some surprising, unexpected, shocking or sad, some triumph or other, some failure. But this was so out of the ordinary. It was, thank God, a kind of bulletin one only gets rarely – if lucky, never – about people in your own circle. It seemed so unlikely after the terrible business of Doug's attempt to hang himself in the theatre.

I am sorry I rang you when I did, out of the blue, but it had been on my mind all day and you were the only one up at the time, and at that point I needed to talk to someone. I started thinking again about how he was one of the people watching Sam when he did his performance. The link shocked me almost as much as the manner of this young man's death. It seems impossible that he could have been there and witnessed something so extraordinary and unique and did what he did then. Did he see it or not? It is not altogether clear. When Sam did the whole play on the stage, I couldn't move, it was such an amazing thing to witness. His timing, the poetry of it, the way he walked, the way he listened, the way he moved was beautiful. It was moving. We will never see anyone play it like that again.

I have been over and over the image of your description of the young man – Doug – sitting on the stage on the day of the dress rehearsal. I had not seen him as particularly troubled. Troubled young people in the theatre are not unusual – particularly among the backstage lot. They pass through the theatre looking for a way into life. That's how it should be. They need to find a way to work, some place, which comes from themselves. Was he in trouble? No trouble can add up to such an act, can it? It was so completely annihilating.

Images of the burning monks came to me. But they are sacrificing their lives to a bigger cause than themselves. I must say that I did think that Doug had a sort of wounded charisma. He was a good-looking man and often silent and broody. But not only that, he was intelligent, thoughtful and hard-working. He could have been someone who would take up a need for justice, not just for himself. He looked like one of those people who dedicate themselves to some political cause and have a capacity to feel for the greater good of others beyond themselves. He was always ready to help, and painstaking in his work. I am thinking now of the pictures of the monks where you can see that they are strong-willed, intelligent people, knowingly ready to kill themselves or be killed if need be. They also give up the solace of ordinary existence, close relationships – family. Doug had no political cause, no society he was laying down his life for as far as I know. It could not have been a political protest. But it must have been a protest and an enraged one at that. There was no note, no clue, just a pile of books in a bag by writers like Gurdjieff and Kierkegaard. He seemed to me to be another lost soul who could not find his way. Could that be enough for his spectacular, awful death by immolation? You can imagine wanting to die, but to be so angry as to want to completely destroy yourself? He must have already destroyed everyone he loved in his mind. I can't help thinking that the entire disturbance around the play was in synchronicity, caught up in the tragedy of this boy's life. Now it seems to make sense. Did you know that artists were painting and drawing apocalyptic visions some time before the outbreak of the World Wars? Remy, a boy, a stagehand who was always citing Jung, said that Jung's psychosis was full of premonitions about the First World War and in synchronicity with it. Did we collectively have a premonition?

The image of us all watching Sam perform the play is such a

powerful one. It fills me with pleasure when I remember it. Now there is another completely different dimension because Doug was there with us. I had a notion that it may have pushed him over the edge. Of course, I know that is ridiculous. Poor Jesse and the baby. What a terrible beginning. Are they in London? No. I am relieved they are far away. It makes it more abstract. Is it cruel of me to say this? It is what I feel. I can visualise that tall, strong, gentle, handsome man standing on the stage or up in the flies. One could see that he did not have a rougher side, only an acute sensitivity. The other men respected him. He did his work with extra diligence. Those passionate eyes; what could have gone wrong? What happened? No one will be able to tell us.

Krapp's tale is not one of despair. He is abject but is also brave. He produces something akin to music which keys straight into our inner, deeper emotional life. It has an ability to look into the resilient soul. Had Doug misread it? Seen something else? Perhaps he did not see anything at all. How could he have misused those words – or the books in his bag – for a blackened, scorched, distorted end?

I talked to Martin later and he gave me a bit of sound comfort. The man must have had some kind of psychotic breakdown. No play could do that. No one thing. The point about Sam's work and all creative work of his depth, he said, is that he can be with the psychotic layer, held by his deep connection to the world through language. Sam can enter into the isolated world of the self and then return to the surface because he never actually leaves it behind. This young man had no such tethering.

Could anyone have seen it coming? I doubt it. Jesse could not have seen it. She was in love and having a baby. She had a different, more mundane vision. I wonder if she did feel the terror. She would have recklessly ignored it if she did. I liked and disliked that in her. I thought of contacting her and then thought better of it. I was told that she was moving back, nearer to her family. They will look after her and the baby – a girl.

It was kind of you also to listen to my concerns about the opera.

I am glad you liked the music as much as I do. Solutions will come out of listening to it again and again.

How are you settling in America? I did not get a chance to ask you last night. I am wondering about working there myself at some point, but I don't know if I could be so far from home.

Much love
Virginia

Acknowledgements

Sincere and personal thanks to my editors at Muswell Press, Ruth Boswell and Jan Woolf, for their tireless work, encouragement and friendship. Also to thank, Cynthia Wild, Serena Nuttall, Hilary Stafford-Clark and Susana Medina, and other friends and writers who read the various drafts. To the members of The Isosceles Theatre Company; Dave Marsden, Pat Abernethy and Jim Dunk, for their work in adapting the book into a play. And to my husband Howard Grey for his constant support of the project.

MORA GREY